"Drink this. It's good for shock."

"I don't like brandy," Anna protested.

"You don't have to like it. This is for medicinal purposes."

Anna drank obediently while she thought about what had happened. Although Gideon had *meant* to frighten her, it hadn't just been a joke—he wasn't that kind of man. Whatever his motives, they stemmed from something a good deal more serious. Anger? Hatred? A desire for vengeance?

LEE WILKINSON lives with her husband in a three-hundred-year-old stone cottage in an English village, which most winters gets cut off by snow. They both enjoy traveling, and recently, joining forces with their daughter and son-in-law, spent a year going around the world "on a shoestring" while their son looked after Kelly, their much-loved German shepherd dog. Her hobbies are reading and gardening and holding impromptu barbecues for her long-suffering family and friends.

Lee Wilkinson

A VENGEFUL DECEPTION

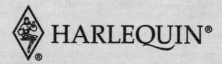

TORONTO • NEW YORK • LONDON
AMSTERDAM • PARIS • SYDNEY • HAMBURG
STOCKHOLM • ATHENS • TOKYO • MILAN • MADRID
PRAGUE • WARSAW • BUDAPEST • AUCKLAND

ISBN 0-373-12264-0

A VENGEFUL DECEPTION

First North American Publication 2002.

This edition published by arrangement with Harlequin Books S.A.

Visit us at www.eHarlequin.com

Printed in U.S.A.

CHAPTER ONE

IT WAS Christmas Eve and, at five o'clock in the afternoon, already dark outside. In the old square, the carefully preserved Victorian street lamps spilled pools of yellow light on to the cobbles.

In line with the bow window of her now empty shop, Anna was stooping to nail down the lid of a wooden packing case.

An occasional glance through the uneven panes had told her that for the last half an hour or so there had been few people about in the square.

Most of the other shops, in what was something of a backwater, were already closed or closing. Only the jewellers and the expensive wine merchants, their windows glittering with tinsel, seemed set to remain open longer.

A sudden pricking in her thumbs, the certainty that someone was standing outside watching her, made Anna glance up sharply. Right on the edge of her vision, a dark figure was moving away.

Shrugging off a feeling of unease, she assured herself that it had no doubt been someone just innocently walking past.

Magnified by the bottle-glass, she could see huge, feathery flakes of snow starting to drift down. She had always loved snow, and the sight brought a touch of magic to an otherwise dismal day.

Bending again to her task, she finished knocking the final nail into the lid of the last packing case, and, putting down her hammer, looked around her with a faint sigh.

Apart from a residue of dust and packing materials, nothing was left. The shelves and the window were bare, as was the dark, cramped office-cum-stockroom at the rear of the tiny Dickensian shop.

Only the slightly musty smell of old paper, leather bindings and printer's ink lingering on the air spoke of books and a dream that had ended.

All the most precious first editions and manuscripts had gone, collected the previous day by the agent who had bought them.

The rest of the stock had been carefully packed into cases that were scheduled to be picked up during the quiet few days between Christmas and New Year.

From the first, Anna's long-cherished ambition to run her own specialist bookshop had been encouraged by her good friend Cleo.

Though complete opposites in both temperament and looks—Anna, tall and slim and dark, a quiet, self-contained girl, Cleo, short and plump and fair, bubbling with life and enthusiasm—the two girls had been friends since they were toddlers.

Throughout their schooldays and college years they had shared nearly all their hopes and fears, their successes and disappointments.

When Anna had finally managed to raise enough capital to rent the shop and add a few antique maps to her small amount of stock, Cleo had been as pleased as Punch.

Though a busy mother with young twins, she had given what practical help she could, and an endless supply of moral support.

But now, after many months of hard work and effort, and mainly due to lack of finance, the venture had sadly ended in defeat.

Cleo, vastly sympathetic but unable to help, had popped into the shop the previous day to lament its closure. 'It's a damned shame. I just wish I could help in some way but, short of winning the lottery... What will you do now?'

Anna had shrugged, trying to appear philosophical. 'As soon as Christmas is over, start looking for a job.'

'It shouldn't be too difficult with your knowledge and qualifications.'

They both knew that the optimism was more than a trifle forced.

Rymington, a small, picturesque market town encircled by hills and quiet, fertile fields, was thriving and affluent. Within easy reach of London, it attracted a stream of seasonal holiday-makers. But jobs, other than in the tourist industry, were few and far between.

It was one of the reasons that had made Anna seize the chance and take over the shop on a short lease, and with what she knew to be barely sufficient capital. There had simply been no other opportunities available.

Despite that lack, she wanted to stay in Rymington where she had been born and brought up. After leaving college, a couple of years spent in London had only reinforced her dislike of big cities, and finally sent her home weary and disillusioned.

'You were so close to making a go of it,' Cleo had mourned. 'If only the lease hadn't come up for renewal.'

But it had. And the considerably higher rent that Deon Enterprises, the new owners of the complex, were demanding had been the last straw.

All that remained of the stock Anna had so painstakingly gathered together had been bought as a job lot by an agent for a private collector.

Knowing she was in a cleft stick, he had beaten her down in price and finally, in desperation, she had been forced to sell at a loss.

Her only consolation was that the sale had raised just enough money to cover her debts, including what she owed the bank, and allow her to walk away with her head held high.

The same way she had walked away from David.

No, she wouldn't think about David. Memory Lane was just a circular route around a lingering pain.

Squaring her shoulders, Anna crossed to the mahogany counter, her footsteps echoing in the emptiness, and, pulling on her coat, picked up her shoulder-bag and the small weekend case that waited there.

When they had exchanged Christmas gifts, Cleo had asked, 'Will you be seeing Paul over the holiday?'

'No,' Anna had answered firmly. 'He wanted me to, but I said I couldn't. I didn't want to raise his hopes.'

'You could do a lot worse.' Cleo, who had introduced the pair, felt she had a vested interest. 'I know he's more than fifteen years older than you, but he's a well-respected barrister, with a *very* nice house, and he's not bad-looking. What more could any girl ask?'

Cleo was so happy with her own marriage that she felt sorry for anyone who didn't share the same blissful state.

'You do like him, don't you?' she persisted.

Resisting the temptation to say, *not particularly*, Anna agreed, 'Yes, he's very nice.'

'And you like children.'

Paul was a widower with a nine-year-old daughter.

'Yes, I like children,' Anna admitted. 'Sophie's a sweet little girl. But that doesn't mean I want to be her step-mother.'

Sighing, Cleo gave up for the time being. 'So what are you planning to do over Christmas?'

'Just have a nice quiet break,' Anna said lightly.

The other girl wasn't fooled for an instant. 'That means you're going to be on your own. Why don't you come to us again? Come for the whole weekend.'

Alan, Cleo's husband, was a quiet, rather shy man, who wasn't fond of company.

'Thanks, but I don't think I will.'

'Don't be silly,' Cleo said, well aware of the reason for the refusal. 'Alan won't object.'

He might not *object*, because he loved his wife and wanted to make her happy, but he wouldn't *like* it.

Though he'd done his best to make Anna welcome the previous year, when she had just moved back to the town, Anna had felt sure he would rather have been alone with his family.

'And the twins will be delighted,' Cleo urged. 'They'll probably get you up at the crack of dawn, but it has to be better than spending a lonely Christmas in a bedsit.'

Troubled by the thought that Cleo might only be asking her out of a sense of duty, and might secretly prefer to have her husband and children to herself, Anna said, 'Thanks a million. But I really won't be lonely. I'll find plenty to do.'

'Well, I won't try to persuade you, but if you change your mind at the last minute, just turn up. The spare room's ready, we've enough food to feed an army, and you'll be more than welcome. Truly.'

And this morning, over her solitary breakfast of toast and coffee, her spirits at their lowest ebb, Anna *had* changed her mind.

Unable to bear the thought of waking on Christmas morning with no happier prospect than a day spent alone in her poky room, she had decided to go to Cleo's after all.

Finding clean undies and several changes of clothing—the twins were expert at spreading chocolate and other sticky substances over everything—she had hastily packed what she would need before setting off for the shop.

Now, case in hand, her bag over her shoulder, she switched off the lights, ducked her smooth, dark head beneath the low lintel, and closed and locked the black-painted door behind her.

Dropping the key into her bag, she looked up at the black sign above the lopsided bow window. The gold lettering read, 'Savanna Sands Rare Books and Manuscripts'.

The leaden feeling of failure and despair that had haunted her for weeks had gone. All she could feel now was empty and hollow.

It was still snowing, the flakes smaller and crisper, starting to stick, covering the uneven cobbles with a white blanket and swirling round the street lamps like motes swimming in the beam of a spotlight.

She pulled her coat collar around her ears and, finding the cobblestones were slippy, walked with care towards the arched passageway that led through to the car park at the rear of the old square.

Built alongside the river, it had once comprised mainly ship's chandlers and warehouses, until a restoration scheme had transformed the complex into a tourist attraction.

After the relative brightness of the square, with its lamps and lighted shop windows, the passageway, and the long, narrow car park which lay between the backs of the shops and the tow-path, were gloomy and ill lit.

There was a scattering of vehicles still parked, but not another soul in sight. Deep patches of shadow lay between each small pool of light.

As Anna unlocked the door of her old Cavalier, a movement she sensed rather than saw made her glance up swiftly.

Through the curtain of falling snow the place appeared to be deserted, yet a sixth sense insisted that someone was lying in wait, watching her, and the fine hairs on the back of her neck rose.

Telling herself she was being a fool, that there was no one there, she tried to shrug off the feeling, but it persisted.

As she peered into the murk, a large black cat, its head turned in her direction, ran along the top of the wall and jumped over into the yard of one of the shops.

Letting out her breath in a sigh of relief, she said aloud, 'There, what did I tell you?'

Tossing her case and bag on to the back seat, she got behind the wheel and turned on the ignition. Cold and damp, the engine took a bit of starting, reminding her that the man at the garage had said she could do with a new battery.

When it finally roared into life, she switched on the windscreen wipers and backed out carefully. Her head-lights, like searching antennae, lit up the whirling snow as she turned towards the exit.

She was just picking up speed when only a few yards ahead a man's dark figure suddenly stepped out from be-tween two parked cars, straight into her path.

Instinctively, she braked and swerved. The wheels skid-ded on the snowy cobbles, and as she struggled to regain control the car slewed sideways before slithering to a halt.

Badly shaken, for a second or two she sat quite still behind the wheel. All she could think was, Thank God she'd missed him.

Or had she?

He'd been very close, and those few split seconds were just a blur. She might have caught him a glancing blow.

Peering out, she could see no sign of him and, with a sick dread that he might be lying injured, she threw open her door and clambered out.

He was slumped on the ground in a patch of deep shadow. A carrier bag, spilling its contents, was lying close by.

As she hurried over to him, to her utmost relief he began to struggle to his feet. 'Are you all right?' she asked anx-iously.

'Fine, I guess… Apart from some minor damage to one arm.' His voice was deep and attractive, an educated voice with a hint of an accent she couldn't quite place.

'Then I *did* hit you? I'm so sorry.'

'Just brushed me. Unfortunately it was enough to make me lose my footing and slip on the cobbles. I landed on my elbow.'

'I'm terribly sorry,' she said again.

'You're not to blame. It was entirely my own fault. I didn't realise you were so close. If I hadn't stepped out in front of you it would never have happened.'

When he'd one-handedly gathered up the carrier and its contents and moved out of the deeper shadow, she was able to make out that he was tall, at least six foot, she judged, and broad across the shoulders.

Despite being marked from their contact with the ground, his well-cut trousers and car-coat were unmistakably expensive.

His left arm appeared to be hanging useless and, concerned, she asked, 'Are you sure you're all right?'

After making an effort to lift it, he admitted, 'I seem to have no use in it at the moment.'

'Perhaps you should go to the Accident and Emergency unit at—'

'On Christmas Eve? Not on your life! No, I'm sure it isn't serious. So long as I'm able to drive.'

'I don't see how you can drive in that state,' she objected.

'You may have a point. In which case I'd better try to find a taxi.' Ruefully, he added, 'I've been in town most of the afternoon and I haven't seen any about, which rather suggests that they might be few and far between.'

He was right. At Your Service, the town's main taxi firm, had recently closed down, and as yet no one had taken their place.

Still feeling she was partly to blame, despite his disclaimer, Anna offered, 'If you like, I'll drive you home.'

'I couldn't possibly put you to so much trouble.'

She shook her head. 'It's the very least I can do. Where do you live?'

'On the Old Castle Road.'

Off hand she couldn't recall any houses on that quiet, country road, apart from the Manor. But it was a while since she'd been that way, and new estates were springing up everywhere.

'Then it really is no trouble,' she said briskly. 'That's the way I'm going.'

It was true that Cleo and her family lived in that general direction, but not nearly so far out of town.

'If that's so, I'll accept your kind offer... Perhaps you'll be good enough to take this while I collect the rest of my provisions?'

As Anna relieved him of the carrier and put it in the back of her own car, he crossed to a dark-coloured Laguna parked close by.

Through the falling snow she watched him fish in his pocket for the keys, open the boot, and with one hand begin to manoeuvre a box of groceries.

It seemed he'd been shopping for his wife.

'Let me.' As soon as the box had joined the other things on the back seat, she invited, 'Jump in.'

As she took her place behind the wheel, he slid in beside her and turned his head to look at her.

He saw a face of enchanting beauty. Long-lashed almond eyes set wide apart—eyes that were the colour of woodsmoke—high cheekbones, a straight nose, and a lovely mouth above a softly rounded chin. Her smooth dark hair, which was taken up in a knot, was spangled with snowflakes.

In the glare of the overhead light she saw him properly for the first time, and what she saw threw her completely.

For a long moment a sense of shock held her rigid. His sidelong glance, the shape of his head and that cleft chin, reminded her of David.

But he wasn't really like David.

His eyes were green, flecked with gold.

David's had been blue.

His hair, when dry, would have the bleached paleness of ripe corn, while in fascinating contrast his brows and lashes were dark.

David's brows and lashes had been as fair as his hair.

His tanned, good-looking face was hard-boned and tough.

David's had been boyishly handsome.

Added to that, this man must be in the region of thirty, where David had been just twenty-two at that time. A year younger than herself.

No, he wasn't like David at all.

Yet his effect on her was just as immediate, just as intense, abruptly destroying her composure and robbing her of any self-assurance.

'Something wrong?' he asked.

'No.' Her voice shook betrayingly as she added, 'Just for a second you reminded me of someone I used to know.'

Turning hastily away, she started the car, and, driving with care, made her way out of the car park.

The town centre was aglow with fairy lights and decorations, the shop windows bright with Christmas cheer. Around the tall tree set up in the Old Market Square, a group from the local church were singing carols and collecting for charity.

There were plenty of people still about, spilling from the shops and stores, laden down with last-minute purchases of gifts and goodies.

The falling snow, which at any other time would have been condemned as an inconvenience, added the final festive touch.

'A picture-postcard scene.'

Her passenger's comment echoed Anna's own thoughts.

'Yes,' she agreed, and because he affected her so strongly found herself talking too much. 'The weather has been very changeable lately. First it was unseasonably mild, then just a couple of days ago we had a severe storm with gale-force winds that did a lot of damage locally. Now this looks like being the first white Christmas we've had for a long time.'

'I ordered it especially,' he told her. 'I love snow, and it's been years since I saw any.'

'Then you don't live in England?'

'I do now. The wanderer has finally returned.'

'Have you been back long?'

'A day or two.'

'From where?'

'The States. After I left college I spent some time travelling the world before settling on America's Western Seaboard. Eventually, having got into computer software, I bought a house on the coast and adopted the Californian lifestyle.'

'Sun, sea, and sand?' Anna murmured.

'In a nutshell.'

'Lucky you.'

'After a while that kind of life can pall. I found I was longing for rural England and the changing seasons. Daffodils and April showers, the smell of summer and new-mown hay, October frosts and decaying leaves, November fogs and log fires... There was nothing particular to keep me in California—my business interests had diversified and become international—so when circumstances gave me the opportunity, I decided to come home.'

He hadn't mentioned a wife, but such an attractive man was almost certain to be married, or at least in some long-term relationship...

Collecting her straying thoughts, she asked, 'And you regard Rymington as home?'

'I was born and bred here.' With deliberation, he added, 'At Hartington Manor, to be exact.'

While keeping her eyes on the road, Anna was aware that he was watching her intently, as though he expected some reaction.

'Hartington Manor? Isn't that where Sir Ian Strange used to live?'

'That's right. I'm Gideon Strange, his son.'

Sir Gideon Strange, and presumably living at the Manor now.

His continued regard made her even more self-conscious, and her voice was jerky as she said, 'I was sorry to hear of your father's death last year.'

'Did you know him?' The question was casual.

'No, not personally. But he's always been well known and highly respected in the town. He did a great deal for charity and local good causes.'

'Yes, he liked to be regarded as a philanthropist.'

There was a suggestion of bitterness in the words.

'I'd half expected him to leave his entire estate to some deserving charity. I could picture the Manor being turned into a home for abused women or stray cats and dogs.'

Then with a quick, sidelong, mocking smile, 'No, I've nothing against either abused women or dumb animals. But though it's too small to count as a stately home, the Manor is a beautiful old place. It would have been a pity to let it go out of the family. There's been a Strange there since Elizabethan times.'

So why on earth would Sir Ian have left it to a charity, rather than his own son?

As though in answer to Anna's unspoken question, Gideon Strange went on, 'I'm afraid my father and I never quite saw eye to eye...'

The judicious wording convinced her that that was an understatement.

'His carefully nurtured public image was somewhat different from the private reality, and I'm afraid he could never forgive me for pointing that out.'

Not knowing quite what to say, Anna kept silent.

After a short pause her companion changed the subject to ask, 'Do you belong to these parts?'

'Yes. In just a minute we'll be passing where I was born and brought up... There... If you can see for the snow? The row of cottages on the right of what used to be the old village green... Ours was the second from the end.'

A lump in her throat, she added, 'I always loved Drum Cottage.' Then swallowing hard, 'Cleo, the friend I'm going to spend Christmas with, used to live next door.'

'No family left?'

'No. My parents and my younger brother died four years ago in a train crash.'

After all this time it still had the power to hurt.

As though he knew, he said, 'Tough.'

Then, after a moment, 'So you're planning to spend Christmas with a friend?'

'Yes. At first I refused the invitation. You see, Cleo's husband isn't fond of company, and I thought I might be intruding... But she said the spare bed was ready and she had enough food to feed an army, so if I changed my mind I was simply to turn up...'

Finding she was babbling again, Anna resolutely closed her mouth.

By now they had reached the outskirts of the town and were bypassing the new estate where Cleo and her family had a neat, semi-detached house.

Leaving the last street lamp behind them, they started to wind their way up Old Castle Hill, the headlights making a tunnel between the trees and picking up the driving white curtain of snow.

'So where do you live now, Anna?'

'I have a bedsit in Grafton Street... What made you call me Anna?' she asked sharply.

There was a barely perceptible pause, before he queried, 'Do you prefer Savanna?'

'No... It's always been shortened to Anna. I mean, how did you know my name?'

'It's on the board above your shop for all to read. Savanna Sands. Very alliterative.'

'How did you know that was my shop?'

'I walked past earlier this afternoon and caught sight of you through the window.'

She frowned. 'What made you presume I was the owner? I could have been anyone.'

'The shop appeared to be empty of stock, and you were wielding a hammer with great determination.'

Before she could point out that he hadn't really answered her question, he went on, 'I rather got the impression that Savanna Sands is due to close down?'

'It's closed,' she said flatly.

'The end of a business, or a dream?'

His percipience was uncanny.

'The latter. Since I was a child I've dreamt of running my very own bookshop.'

'So what happened? Not enough customers, or not enough cash?'

'Both. Tourist trade picks up in the summer, but I couldn't wait till then. My overdraft was stretched to the limit, the lease was up, and the new owners of the building had doubled the rent.'

'What will you do now?'

It was the same question Cleo had asked.

Anna gave the same answer. 'As soon as Christmas is over, start looking for a job.'

'An assistant in a bookshop maybe?'

Stung, she said, 'I'm a qualified librarian.'

Out of the corner of her eye she saw him raise a well-marked brow, before he murmured, 'Really?'

'Yes, really.'

'In a town this size I can't imagine there are boundless opportunities, even for a qualified librarian?'

Hearing the mockery behind the politely phrased question, she made a point of not answering.

'Of course, there's always London,' he pursued. 'Or perhaps you feel a big city isn't for you?'

He had the smooth abrasiveness of pumice-stone.

'I know it isn't. I lived and worked in London after I left college, and I was glad to leave it.'

'You worked in a library?'

She shook her head. 'I had a job as a secretary.'

'But you were still keeping your dream alive.'

Though it was a statement rather than a question, she found herself answering, 'Yes. At weekends, and in my spare time, I went to salerooms and auctions to try and collect together enough rare manuscripts and first editions to start my own business.'

'An expensive undertaking, even for a well-paid secretary,' he commented drily.

'I had some capital.' Annoyed that she'd let herself be provoked into telling a perfect stranger so much, she relapsed into silence, concentrating on her driving.

At the top of the long hill they skirted a bare spinney, where as a child she'd gathered wild primroses, before turning on to Old Castle Road.

The lights of Rymington, below them now and to their left, had vanished, blotted out by the falling snow. It was coming faster now, the wipers having a job to keep the windscreen clear.

Glancing to the right, Anna glimpsed the old red-brick wall of the Manor. The darkness and the conditions made it difficult to judge distances, but they couldn't be too far away from the main gates.

Apparently reading her thoughts, her companion broke the silence to say, 'Only a hundred yards or so to go. You'll see the entrance in a moment.'

Just as he spoke, the headlights picked it up.

Anna had only ever seen the tall, wrought-iron gates closed. Now they stood wide open.

As she drove carefully through them and up the long, winding, unlit drive between tall trees, she remarked, 'The weather seems to be getting worse. I expect your wife will be relieved to see you back.'

'What makes you presume I'm married?'

'Well…with all the shopping and everything…'

'Even poor bachelors have to eat.' He was undoubtedly laughing at her.

A shade stiffly, she said, 'Of course.'

Through the snow the headlights picked up the bulk of a house and flashed across dark windows. It appeared to be deserted.

But of course it couldn't be. A place the size of Hartington Manor was bound to have staff.

Yet, if there were servants, why had he been doing his own shopping?

She brought the car to a halt, and, remembering his injured arm, asked, 'Can I help with the groceries?'

'I'd be grateful if you would.'

Turning off the engine, she made to clamber out.

'May I suggest that you wait here for a moment while I open the door and put on some lights? Normally the security lights would have been working, but the storm you mentioned earlier put an electricity substation out of action. We do have an emergency generator, but unfortunately it has only a very limited capacity.'

He retrieved the carrier, and she watched him walk through the snow to the house. Awkward, one-handed, he held the bag tucked beneath his arm while he felt in his pocket for the key and opened the door.

A moment later, the hall lights and a lantern above the door flashed on.

Switching off the car lights to save the battery, Anna lifted out the box and followed him into the house.

Shouldering the door shut against the snow blowing in, he led the way across a high, panelled hall, and into a large kitchen with a flagged floor and a massive inglenook fireplace.

In front of the hearth, where a log fire was already laid, were a couple of easy chairs and a small, sturdy table.

Beneath a deep shelf that held a gleaming array of copper saucepans and kettles was an Aga, which threw out a welcoming warmth. Around it, fitted in with care, marrying the old to the new, there was every modern convenience.

The only things missing seemed to be servants.

Anna put the box down on a long oak table and turned to the door.

'Before you rush off,' Gideon said, 'I've a proposition to put to you.'

Watching her freeze, he added sardonically, 'Oh, nothing improper, I assure you. It's simply this: you're in need of a job, and I'm in need of an experienced secretary-cum-librarian.'

Wondering if this was his idea of a joke, she looked at him warily.

'Let me briefly explain. The internet gives me all the access I need to world markets, and enables me to buy and sell goods, services, whatever... So as soon as I'm properly

established here, I intend to run my various business interests from home... Hence the need for a secretary.'

'And a librarian?'

'Hartington Manor has a very fine library, as you may
well know.'

She half shook her head.

'But for a while now it's been somewhat neglected. I'd
like to see it put in order and properly catalogued. With
regard to salary, I thought something in the region of...'
He named a sum that no one in their right mind could have
turned down.

When she merely stared at him, he added, 'I hope you
see that as reasonable?'

The slight edge to his tone made her wonder if he was
waiting for some sign of gratitude or enthusiasm.

Before she could find her voice, however, he went on,
'If you accept the post, I'd like you to start work straight
after the holiday.'

There was a silence in which the confusion of her
thoughts was barely contained.

Then, feeling the need to say *something* without com-
mitting herself, she asked the first thing that came into her
head. 'How big is the library?'

'Quite large by private standards.' He dangled the bait.
'Why don't you have a look?'

She took it. 'I'd like to.'

Even if she didn't accept the job, the opportunity to have
a quick look at the Manor's library was one she couldn't
miss.

'Then please feel free.'

He made no immediate move to take her and, somewhat
at a loss, she waited.

It appeared that his thoughts were straying, because it
was a few seconds before he said, 'If you come with me,
I'll show you where the library is.'

He led her back across the hall, past an imposing central staircase on one side of which—rather incongruously, she thought—stood a large brass gong, and, opening one of the double oak doors at the rear, switched on the lights.

'I'm afraid it's not very warm in here. The central heating is electric, so at the moment it's not working.'

Casually, he added, 'You could probably do with a hot cup of tea? I know I could, so I'll go and put the kettle on while you take a look around.'

With a little smile, he closed the door quietly behind him and left her to it.

CHAPTER TWO

THE library was a high, handsome room, with a large stone fireplace and mullioned windows. On every wall there were shelves from floor to ceiling, filled with an array of books that delighted Anna's heart.

At first glance everything seemed to be well cared for. She could discern none of the neglect that Gideon Strange had mentioned.

In one corner was a little pulpit-staircase. It was made of dark oak and beautifully carved; a polished handrail supported by banisters followed the spiral of the steps.

She went over to it and found it moved easily on hidden castors. Slipping off her boots, she climbed the smooth treads and found she could reach the top shelf of books with ease.

Working here would be a pleasure.

But did she want to work for Gideon Strange?

One half of her wanted to very much, but the sensible half warned against it.

Perhaps because of a fancied resemblance to David, there was a physical attraction that made being with him disturbing, to say the least. But could she afford to turn down a chance that, had her prospective employer been anyone else, she would have jumped at?

Perhaps if she asked for a few days to consider his offer? By the time Christmas was over she might feel differently, be able to face the thought of working for him with equanimity.

But who was she trying to fool? He was too charismatic,

too strong a personality, altogether too *dangerous* for her peace of mind.

Though she'd only seen him relatively briefly, that tough, handsome face, with its breathtaking charm and more than a hint of arrogance, was etched indelibly on her mind.

The green eyes, long and narrow and heavily lashed; the chiselled mouth—oh, that mouth!—firm and clean-cut, a fascinating combination of strength and sensuality.

Rather like David's, but with added maturity.

No, she was wrong. David's mouth, while charming, had totally lacked that strength. It might even have been a little weak.

To her great surprise she realised that David had suddenly become shallow and lightweight compared to Gideon Strange...

Which only stiffened her resolve to refuse his offer. Having been badly burnt once had made her wary. He had the kind of explosive sexuality that made her want to run, and keep running...

A soft patter of snow being dashed against the windows drew her attention. The plum velvet curtains were open, and through the darkness pressing against diamond-leaded panes she could see the white flakes scurrying past.

It seemed the wind was rising.

If she didn't leave quite soon she might have difficulty getting back to Cleo's, where everything was light and bright and modern, and the only books were dog-eared paperbacks jostling for space on chipboard shelves.

She descended the steps carefully, put on her boots and, after switching off the lights, hurried back to the kitchen.

The shopping had been unpacked and the thick folk-weave curtains drawn across the windows. A bunch of mistletoe with gleaming white berries lay on the draining board.

Still wearing his jacket, and looking even taller and

broader than she remembered, Gideon Strange was putting tea things on a tray. His fair hair, she noticed, was a little rumpled and quite wet.

Glancing up, he said easily, 'Ah, there you are. The tea's already made.'

Just the sight of him, the sound of his voice, told her that she hadn't been mistaken about his intense attraction. Well, she wouldn't be caught in *that* trap again. She had shed too many tears over David to want to repeat the experience.

'Thanks, but I really haven't time,' she said briskly.

His tone studiously casual, he refused to take no for an answer. 'Just a quick cup before you go. You must be more than ready for one.'

She was, but anxiety to escape, to get on her way, was her prime consideration.

'Milk and sugar?' he asked politely.

'Just a little milk, please.'

Seeing him fumble one-handed to open a four-pint plastic bottle of milk, she said, 'Let me.'

Watching her deftly undo the top, remove the seal and half fill a jug, he said reflectively, 'I could do with you staying until I get the use back in this blasted arm.'

'But surely you can't be on your own here?'

Without answering, he poured out two cups of tea and, handing her one, suggested, 'Why don't you sit down for a minute?'

Remaining standing, she protested, 'You must have servants? I mean, in a place this size...' Her voice tailed off helplessly.

'In the normal way of things there's a full staff, of course. But the Manor hasn't been occupied since my father died. Only Mary Morrison, who was my father's secretary, and her husband Arthur, who used to be the chauffeur, stayed on. They've lived here since before I was born, so they regard it as their home—'

'But if your father's secretary still lives here, why do you need to engage another one?'

Without a flicker of an eyelid, he answered, 'Because Mary is turned sixty and looking forward to a quiet life rather than a full-time job.'

When Anna said nothing further, he went on, 'The Morrisons haven't had a holiday this year, and they wanted to go up to Scotland to spend Christmas and New Year with Arthur's sister. I wasn't expecting to be back in time for Christmas, so I told them to close up the house and go ahead.'

More than a little surprised by his long-winded explanation—it didn't seem to be his style at all—she asked, 'Then there's no one else here?'

'No, indeed.' With soft emphasis he added, 'We're quite alone.'

His words seemed to hold more than a hint of satisfaction, and she felt a sudden disquiet. She'd been on edge from the start, but this was different.

Repressing a shiver brought on by apprehension, Anna warned herself not to let her imagination run riot.

Yet something in his manner, and the knowledge that they were quite alone, was far from reassuring. It must be a good half-mile to the road, and a great deal more than that to the nearest house...

Resolutely pushing away that alarming thought, she reminded herself firmly that Gideon Strange was the son of a well-respected baronet, and the new owner of Hartington Manor.

Of course he posed no threat, had no designs on her. Why on earth should he? She was just a stranger who, because of the circumstances, had given him a lift home, and to whom he'd offered a job.

If there were any more *personal* feelings, they were on her side... Which was why she'd decided not to accept his offer.

As though he could see into her mind, he said, 'I take it you've come to a decision?'

'Y-you mean about the job?' she stammered. 'Well, I...' Then, chickening out, knowing it would be a lot easier to say no from the other end of a telephone, she lied, 'I—I'd like a chance to think it over, if you don't mind.'

His green eyes glinted. 'I actually meant about staying here. Don't you think, as we're both on our own, that it would be nice if we were to spend Christmas together?'

Trying to believe he was teasing, she answered as lightly as possible, 'Thanks for the offer, but I couldn't *possibly* stay.'

Finishing her tea as quickly as she could, she put her cup back in the saucer with a little rattle, and, striving to sound casual, remarked, 'Cleo will be wondering where on earth I've got to.'

Dark brows lifted a fraction. 'I understood you to say she wasn't expecting you?'

Cursing herself for telling him so much, Anna said weakly, 'She knows me well enough to be certain I'd change my mind. Now I really must be going. They eat about seven, as soon as the twins have gone to bed...'

'Well, if I can't persuade you to stay,' he murmured regretfully, 'I'll see you to the door.'

At that instant the lights flickered and went out.

Anna's gasp was audible.

'Don't worry.' In the darkness, Gideon's voice sounded unconcerned. 'It's the generator. I'm afraid it's on the blink. If you stay where you are for a moment, I'll find a candle.'

Just as he finished speaking, the lights flashed on again, brilliant after the momentary blackness.

With a feeling of relief she hurried out of the kitchen

and, trying belatedly to look as if she wasn't *escaping*, crossed the hall to the front door.

Though she'd had several seconds' start, and Gideon didn't appear to be moving quickly, he was there before her.

His back to the dark wood, blocking her way, he said, 'Let me know about the job, won't you?'

'Yes… Yes, I will.'

'Oh, just one more thing…'

She paused and looked up at him. Close to, he dwarfed her five feet seven inches, and his shoulders seemed as wide as a barn door.

He lifted his right hand over their heads and, before she could react to the sprig of mistletoe he held, bent his head and kissed her on the lips.

For a few endless seconds she stood transfixed while that firm mouth covered hers, making her heart race and her head spin. Then, jerking away as though she'd been scalded, she brushed past him and pulled open the door.

She was shocked to find everywhere was white-over and a full-scale blizzard had started to blow. Snowflakes gusted in, swirling round their heads like handfuls of icy confetti.

'I think it would be extremely unwise to set off in conditions like these,' Gideon advised evenly.

Panic-stricken at the thought of having to stay, she insisted, 'I'll be all right, really I will. I don't have too far to go.'

Disturbed, almost *shocked* by the effect of that relatively innocent kiss, she knew wild horses would have had a job to keep her there.

'Well, do take care.'

Ducking her head, she made her way through the driving white curtain to the car.

Standing in the doorway, Gideon called after her, 'Goodnight, Anna, and a merry Christmas.'

Somehow she managed, 'Thank you, and the same to you.'

Slamming the car door behind her, she fastened her seat belt and felt for the keys which she'd left in the ignition.

Though the lights came on feebly, proving it wasn't the battery, the engine flatly refused to start.

'Try it without the lights,' Gideon shouted, appearing at the car window.

She tried repeatedly, without success and with growing desperation.

Opening the car door a crack, he remarked cheerfully, 'It doesn't seem to be firing.'

Endeavouring to speak calmly, she asked, 'Is there anything you can do?'

'I'm sorry to say I don't know much about machinery.' Humorously, he added, 'When I tried tinkering with the generator I only seemed to make matters worse.'

In an odd kind of way his answer surprised her. She had put him down as a man who would be able to deal with almost anything.

'You don't have another car, I suppose?' She was clutching at straws.

'I'm afraid not. All the family cars were sold after my father died.'

Freezing snow was blowing in, settling on her hair, making her shiver. 'Then it will have to be a taxi.'

'I doubt if any taxis will continue to run in these conditions.'

'It's quite likely that the main roads will still be clear. Please will you phone for me?'

'Sorry. That isn't possible.'

'Why isn't it possible?' she asked sharply.

'Because the phone isn't working. The gales blew down several trees, which in turn brought down the line...' He was having to shout, the wind whipping away his words.

'I gather it will be after Christmas before they get round to mending it.'

'Haven't you got a mobile phone?' Most people had these days. Though of course he was newly over from the States…

Opening the door fully, he said, 'Yes, I hired one. But unfortunately I wasn't thinking, and I left it in my car.' Then, briskly, 'Now, may I suggest you come back inside, before we both freeze to death?'

For one mad moment she toyed with the idea of setting off on foot, until common sense reminded her that it must be something in the region of five miles back to where Cleo lived.

It would be unwise, to say the least, to attempt to walk that far at night and in a raging blizzard, wearing high-heeled fashion boots.

Fate, it seemed, was against her.

Seeing nothing else for it, she clambered out.

'I expect you'll be wanting these.' Reaching over, he used his right hand to gather up her bag and case from the rear seat, then leaned against the car door to close it.

Head down against the driving snow, her teeth clenched to stop them chattering, Anna followed him back to the house.

The air inside felt almost as cold as the outside, and a drift of snow, blown in through the partly open door, powdered the dark oak floorboards.

Using his foot to shut the door behind them, Gideon remarked, 'As I said earlier, the central heating isn't working, so with an Aga that runs on either gas or solid fuel, the warmest place in the house is the kitchen.'

He led the way back there and, putting her belongings on an old settle, shrugged out of his wet jacket and hung it on one of a row of large, wooden pegs.

'Let me.' Having one-handedly helped her off with her

coat, he hung it beside his own, before finding a couple of towels. 'Better dry your hair. You don't want to catch a chill.'

He rubbed his own head then, leaving the towel hanging around his neck, crossed to the huge fireplace, both sides of which were stacked with kindling, split logs and sawn-off branches the size of young trees.

Anna dried her face. Her cheeks felt stiff and frozen, her ears were numb, and she could tell her nose was red.

While she removed the pins and rubbed her long, dark hair, she watched him take a match from the box, strike it with a flick of his thumbnail, and crouch on his haunches to light the kindling.

Then, his right hand flat on the stone hearth, he leaned forward to blow the faltering flame into life.

She noticed that he wore a heavy gold signet-ring on his fourth finger, before her eyes were drawn to his handsome profile.

Once again she saw a sneaking likeness to David.

But while David's profile had been just as handsome, it had had nothing of the ruthless quality that this man's possessed.

Using both hands to pull back her still damp hair, she knotted it loosely in the nape of her neck, while a shiver ran through her that had nothing to do with the cold.

What on earth was she going to do, stranded here alone with this disturbing stranger?

Her practical streak pointed out that there wasn't much she *could* do. Somehow she would have to pull herself together and make the best of things. At least until the blizzard stopped.

But even if it did stop she wouldn't be able to leave until morning, and the thought of having to spend the night here was a nerve-racking one, to say the least...

Glancing up, he said sardonically, 'There's no need to

look *quite* so scared. I only turn into a werewolf at full moon.'

She was hoping he couldn't see the colour that his words had whipped into her cheeks, when he added, 'Come and get warm by the fire.'

Chilled to the bone, needing no more urging, Anna went over to stand in front of the huge fireplace where the logs were blazing merrily and already starting to throw out a comforting heat.

Watching him use his right hand to pull up an easy chair for her, Anna felt a sudden shame that she'd thought only of herself and not of him. His elbow must have taken a nasty knock, and if the life was starting to come back into it he might well be in considerable pain.

'Would you like me to take a look at your arm? If you have a first aid box, it's possible there may be some liniment, or something that would help to ease any—'

'I'm sure you'd make a charming nurse,' he broke in smoothly, 'but it really isn't necessary. It will no doubt be good as new by morning. Now, I propose we have an aperitif, while I rustle us up something to eat.'

On edge and apprehensive, Anna had never felt less like eating. But no doubt he was hungry.

'Perhaps I'd better do it?' she offered.

'My cooking's not that bad,' he said drily.

'I was thinking of your arm.'

'Don't worry, I'll make it a one-handed job. But before I start, is there anything in particular that you dislike?'

'No, I like most things.'

'I was considering a stir-fry, if that suits you? Everything comes in ready-to-use packs, which simplifies matters, and we can eat it on our knees in front of the fire.'

'A stir-fry sounds fine.'

Having discarded the towel, he produced a bottle of sherry, a bottle of white wine and a corkscrew.

'There is something you can do, after all. Opening bottles seems to require two hands.'

The lights, which weren't over-bright at the best of times, flickered and went out, leaving only the firelight.

As Anna stood irresolute they flashed on again, and she breathed a sigh of relief. Firelight alone made things much too *intimate* for her peace of mind.

When both bottles had been opened, Gideon put the wine on one side and poured the pale amber sherry. Passing her a glass, he said, 'I hope you like it fairly dry?'

'Yes, thank you.' She didn't drink alcohol as a rule, but this seemed no time to say so.

Returning to her chair, she stretched her feet to the blaze and sipped her sherry. Covertly, from beneath long, dark lashes, she watched him assemble the ingredients for a stir-fry, and put a wok to heat on the Aga.

He was wearing a cream cable-knit sweater that emphasised the width of his chest and shoulders. His corn-coloured hair was rumpled, and a single lock had fallen over his forehead, making him look disarmingly boyish.

Which she was quite sure he was *not*.

He was a mature and dangerous man, and she would do well to remember that, rather than allow herself to be lulled into a false sense of security...

As the unaccustomed sherry and the warmth of the fire banished the chill from her bones, Anna began to relax and try to take a more rational view of the situation.

Though she didn't *like* being stranded here alone with Gideon Strange, things weren't really *that* desperate.

She had food and warmth and a roof over her head and, as she'd reminded herself earlier, he was a man of some standing, and no doubt perfectly trustworthy.

He might have kissed her under the mistletoe, but on Christmas Eve that could hardly be counted as a crime. And honesty made her admit that, had it been any other man, she wouldn't have given the kiss a second thought.

Because he reminded her of David, and brought to life all the feelings she had worked so hard to stifle, she was tense and hypersensitive.

Which made the prospect of having to spend the rest of the evening in his company a daunting one.

But rather than let it throw her, what she must do was stay calm and unmoved. Or at least *appear* to.

If by any chance he did make a pass at her, she could quietly freeze him off. After all, past boyfriends had re-marked with some bitterness that it was something she was good at! And though he might not relish having to take no for an answer, she couldn't see him forcing himself on any woman.

He wouldn't need to. A man such as he was more likely to have to fight off eager females.

It seemed strange that he wasn't married. Perhaps he was the 'love 'em and leave 'em' type? Or maybe he preferred a live-in lover? She couldn't see a man with such an aura of sexuality living like a monk.

But if he was involved in any kind of serious, long-term relationship, why had he returned home alone? Unless his partner planned to follow...

'The best thing about a stir-fry is that it doesn't take too long.'

Gideon's voice broke into Anna's thoughts and, startled, she looked up to find him by her side. He was holding a small round tray which he settled on her knees. It held a napkin, a glass of wine, a bowl heaped with chicken, prawns and colourful vegetables, and a pair of chopsticks.

He put the bottle containing the remaining wine on the low table, and a moment later, equipped with a matching tray, took his seat opposite.

Raising his glass, so the flickering flames turned the colourless wine to gold, he said, 'Here's to us!'

She drank dutifully.

'A stir-fry may not be particularly appropriate,' he admitted with a grin, 'but tuck in while it's nice and hot.'

Suddenly finding she was hungry after all, she needed no more urging.

For a while they ate in silence, then, picking up the bottle of wine, he leaned forward to refill her glass.

She shook her head. 'No more for me, thank you.'

'Sure you won't have another glass? After all, it is Christmas Eve.'

'I don't think so, thanks,' she refused politely. 'I don't usually drink.'

'How virtuous of you.'

Ignoring the blatant mockery, she concentrated on her food. It was surprisingly good, and when her bowl was empty she looked up to say, 'Thank you very much. I enjoyed that.'

'Tomorrow we'll stick with traditional Christmas fare— turkey, stuffing, and all the trimmings. I even remembered to buy cranberry sauce,' he added triumphantly.

When she said nothing, he quirked an eyebrow at her. 'Don't you think congratulations are in order?'

'I expect to be gone by tomorrow morning.' Her voice was unconsciously edgy.

'Listening to that wind howling, and the snow beating against the windows, I shouldn't bet on it. I remember a similar blizzard when I was a boy,' he went on reminiscently. 'Because the drive dips in several places, and the contours of the land encourage drifting, we were snowed in for several days. Still, if we *are* snowbound, we've plenty of food and drink and a good supply of logs, so there's nothing to worry about. We're lucky, really.'

It was pretty much what she'd told herself earlier, but

hearing him sound so glib and self-satisfied touched her on the raw.

Suddenly, he started to chuckle.

It was a deep, attractive sound that at any other time would have made her want to laugh with him. Now, she protested stiffly, 'I really don't see anything to laugh at.'

'You're not sitting where I am. If you could see your face!'

Her grey eyes sparkling with anger, she pointed out, 'It's all right for you. You're at home, where you *want* to be.'

'Do I take it you'd sooner be sitting alone in a bedsit? Or inflicting yourself on a family who may not really want you?'

Cheeks burning, Anna wished, not for the first time, that she hadn't told him so much. She wasn't usually so forthcoming. It had been sheer nervousness that had made her babble on.

'I'm sorry,' he said after a moment. 'That wasn't particularly kind.'

She grasped the nettle. 'No, but it doesn't stop it being true.'

'Actually, I doubt if it is. Put it down to pique on my part, because I'm very happy with the way things have turned out.'

When, flustered, she said nothing, he went on, 'If you were born and bred here, you must have plenty of close friends?'

'After I left school I was away at college for three years, and then I lived in London for two. I lost touch with most of them.'

'Well, if there's nothing spoiling, so to speak, I don't see why you're so desperate to get away. I know that at the moment the Manor has a distinct lack of creature comforts, but I was hoping you might have enough spirit to be able to regard being marooned here as fun, a kind of adventure…'

That was how she *would* have regarded it, had the man been any other than himself.

But she could hardly tell him that.

Eyes gleaming between those fascinating long lashes, he went on with mock sympathy, 'But I guess the whole thing must be terribly unnerving, especially when the lights keep going out—'

As though on cue, the lights flickered and dimmed, before brightening again.

'—and you're stranded in the dark with a man you know absolutely nothing about. A man who could be *anything* or *anybody*…'

Well aware by now that she was being teased, she smiled and said, 'It's not quite that bad. After all, I know you're Sir Ian's son, and the new master of Hartington Manor.'

'Well, now you're satisfied that I pose no threat—'

'I didn't say that.' The words were out before she could prevent them.

Green eyes alight with laughter, he glanced at the mistletoe, which he'd hung from a hook on the beamed ceiling. 'Ah! Well, perhaps if I burn the mistletoe?'

It was clear that he'd noticed her reaction to his kiss. But then an experienced man such as he could hardly have failed to.

Blushing furiously, she said, 'I hardly think it's necessary to *burn* it.'

'You mean if I just refrain from making use of it?' He sighed deeply. 'A pity, really, as it's the festive season. Still, if that's what it takes to make you feel happy and secure… Now, would you like anything else to eat? Fruit? Cheese? Christmas cake?'

'Nothing else, thank you,' she said primly.

'Then I'll make some coffee.'

While he filled a cafétière and set a tray with sugar, cream and fine bone-china cups, she thought about what had just been said.

In an odd sort of way, bringing things into the open had eased the tension and created a more friendly atmosphere.

His whole attitude had shown clearly that any problem had been on her side. But then she'd known that from the start. It had been her reaction to him that had made things so uncomfortable...

'If you'd be so kind...?'

Glancing up, anticipating his need, she pulled the small table into place.

Sliding the tray on to it, he asked, 'How do you like your coffee?'

'A little cream, please. No sugar.'

She noticed he took his own black, with neither cream nor sugar.

While they drank, they sat staring into the leaping flames and listening to the sizzle of snowflakes falling down the chimney on to the burning logs.

The silence had become easy, almost companionable, and the prospect of spending the rest of the evening in his company was no longer quite so daunting.

When their cups were empty, Gideon asked cheerfully, 'Now, what shall we do until bedtime?'

'Perhaps I'd better start by washing up.'

He shook his head. 'We have a dishwasher when there's sufficient electricity to run it. I meant what shall we do by way of entertainment? There's television, of course, but the living-room is bound to be as cold as charity, and I'm not sure that the generator will take the strain.'

Anna shook her head. 'I don't care much for television. I've always preferred books.'

'I'm with you there! Well, if it's books you want, there are certainly plenty of those. Apart from the library itself, my father half filled the study with his own personal collection of first editions.'

'Really?'

'Though I'm not particularly knowledgeable on the subject,' Gideon added levelly, 'it's an interest I share. So if you'd care to see the collection some time, I'll be happy to show you.'

The offer was made casually, but she answered with undisguised eagerness, 'Thank you. I'd like that.'

'As you may imagine, going through catalogues and suchlike took up a great deal of time; that's why Mary Morrison became his secretary.'

'I'd no idea that your father was a collector,' Anna remarked.

Just for an instant she saw a look that might have been angry disbelief on Gideon's face, then it was gone.

'You astonish me,' he said coolly. 'I'd always presumed it was common knowledge, at least among the people who knew him reasonably well.'

'As I said earlier I *didn't* know him personally. I just knew *of* him.'

'All the same,' Gideon persisted, 'as you and he were presumably *competitors* in the same market, I would have expected you to have at least heard his name mentioned in that connection.'

Wondering why it mattered, why he was making an issue of it, she shook her head. 'Not necessarily. You see, if it becomes known that a wealthy collector is interested in a certain item it can push the price sky-high, so a lot of the more serious collectors find it better to buy through an agent rather than get involved on a personal level.'

She couldn't tell whether she'd convinced him or not. His face was expressionless, his green eyes hard and opaque as jade, hiding his thoughts.

After a moment, he shrugged and admitted lightly, 'That

makes sense, I suppose. Buying and selling is business, whatever commodity is involved.'

She was pleased that finally he seemed to have accepted what she'd told him.

Still the puzzle remained—why had he looked as though he disbelieved her in the first place? What possible reason could she have for lying about a thing like that?

CHAPTER THREE

ALL at once a log slipped and rolled on to the hearth in a shower of bright sparks. Gideon got to his feet and used a large pair of tongs to replace it.

Having resumed his seat, he gave her a lopsided smile that did strange things to her breathing and pulse rate before remarking, 'Now, after getting sidetracked, suppose we continue with our discussion?'

Wits scattered, she said vaguely, 'Our discussion?'

'If you remember, we were trying to decide on our evening's fun. We've just dismissed television, so that rules out two possibilities...'

'Two?'

He gave a sideways glance at the mistletoe, then watched with undisguised amusement while the colour rose in her cheeks.

Gritting her teeth, she asked as evenly as possible, 'Are there any playing cards? Or a chess set, perhaps?'

'There used to be, but I've no idea whether they still exist.' His face suddenly wintry, he went on, 'The only games my father enjoyed playing were with women... Or rather with a succession of girls, most of whom were young enough to be his daughter.'

Catching sight of her expression, he commented, 'You look surprised.'

'I am.' Without thinking about it, she had always presumed that Sir Ian was the epitome of respectable upper-class morality.

The green eyes pinned her. 'Then you had no idea?'

Shaking her head, she said, 'No.'

'Now it's my turn to be surprised. Though he was always very careful to be discreet, more often than not that kind of thing gets about, and mud sticks, especially in a small town like Rymington.'

Again she shook her head. 'I've never heard a word breathed against him.'

Gideon shrugged, and changed the subject to query casually, 'How much of Hartington Manor have you seen?'

Wondering why he was asking when he knew quite well, she answered, 'The hall, the kitchen, and the library.'

'You haven't seen the rest of this wing, or the older part?'

'No. I didn't know there *was* an older part.'

'It's quite spooky,' he said with relish. 'There are sliding panels and a secret passage. I'll show you round if you like. It's just the sort of thing to do on a dark and snowy Christmas Eve.'

Anna found herself wondering if he was trying to wind her up. Or had he perhaps, in his youth, read too many adventure yarns?

Perhaps her expressive face gave away what she was thinking, because he grinned at her and added, 'Then we'll come back and sit round the fire and tell each other true-life ghost stories.'

Carefully, she said, 'I'm afraid I don't know any true-life ghost stories.'

'No personal experience? You've never actually met a ghost?'

'Not to my knowledge. But then that's hardly surprising, considering where I've lived. You can't expect any self-respecting ghost to bother haunting a tiny three-bedroomed cottage or a bedsit.'

'Yes, I can quite see it might cramp their style. Whereas a place of this size...' He paused, waiting for her to ask.

Widening her eyes, she obliged. 'You mean Hartington Manor has a real live ghost?'

He gave a pained frown. 'I can see you don't take the matter seriously.'

'Should I?'

'Oh, definitely. We can't have Sir Roger upset.'

'Sir Roger?'

'Sir Roger Strange. But I'll tell you all about him later... Now, are you game?'

'I suppose so,' she agreed a shade doubtfully. There was something about his manner, the glint in his eye, that she didn't altogether trust.

'Then let's get started.' He got to his feet and offered a hand to pull her up.

Pretending she hadn't seen it, she rose obediently.

'It's bound to be cold,' he remarked, 'so we'd better have our coats.'

He lifted Anna's down and held it one-handed while she slipped it on, before shrugging into his own jacket. 'And we'll need a candle and some matches to take with us.'

Wondering what he was up to, she asked, 'But surely the lights will work?'

'Oh, yes, if the generator holds out. But not all the house has been modernised, so we'll need the candle for later.'

Trying to sound merely practical, she asked, 'Wouldn't it make more sense to go when it's daylight?'

'What, and spoil the fun?'

'I think you're trying to scare me.'

Instead of denying it, he asked, 'Am I succeeding?'

'No,' she said firmly.

Collecting the matches, he dropped them into his jacket pocket. Then, while she watched with growing misgivings, he crossed to the huge dresser and picked up a beautifully ornate candlestick.

Made of black wrought iron, it was fashioned in the form

of a dragon standing on clawed feet, while its tail curled to form a handgrip and its raised wings and open mouth held the candle.

'Perhaps you wouldn't mind carrying it for the moment?' he asked politely.

She took it from him and found it was surprisingly heavy.

'Now, shall we start in the basement?' He turned to lead the way.

They went through a small door at the end of the hall and descended a flight of worn stone steps. There was a wide stone passage which branched off into a series of storerooms and sculleries.

Opening the door into a large, stone-flagged room, Gideon told her, 'This used to be the kitchen, while the present kitchen was once the servants' hall.'

Peering in, Anna saw deep stone sinks, a scrubbed oak table flanked by massive dressers and, in the huge fireplace, an old iron spit, big enough to roast a whole ox.

It was so cold their breath made a white vapour on the air, and she wasn't sorry when he switched out the light and moved on.

At the end of the passage, another flight of steps led up to the main living quarters. A peep into the various rooms showed they were elegantly furnished, with beautiful wall-papers, ornately plastered ceilings, and everything neces-sary to gracious living.

'As you can see this part of the house has been altered and brought up to date as much as possible, without spoil-ing the old place. It used to be quite comfortable, and no doubt will be again when the heating's working,' he added dryly.

'On the floor above, apart from the Morrisons' self-contained flat, there are seven bedrooms and various bathrooms, but there's nothing much of interest, so I won't take you upstairs until we go to bed.'

His words were innocent enough on the surface, but there was something, some nuance, that made every nerve-ending in her body tighten.

'This archway leads through to the East Wing,' he went on smoothly. 'It hasn't been lived in for donkey's years, and it's by far the most interesting. There's neither gas nor electricity, so this is where we'll need to light the candle.' Taking it from her, he went on, 'The matches are in my right-hand pocket, if you'd be kind enough to fish them out.'

Feeling in his pocket seemed somehow so *personal* that Anna had to brace herself to do it.

Judging by the mocking gleam in his eye, he knew exactly how she felt, and was enjoying her discomfort.

As she stepped closer, she fancied she could feel the warmth emanating from his body, and shivered in response.

The box located, she struck a match and lit the candle he was holding. She was annoyed to find that her hand shook.

'Something bothering you?' he asked innocently.

Hurriedly blowing out the match before it burnt her fingers, she replaced the box in his pocket, and answered, 'I'm cold.' It wasn't a complete lie.

The candle held high, making black leaping shadows on the walls, he led her down a flight of stone steps and into the East Wing.

There were frequent changes of direction and level, two steps up here, three down there, and what seemed to be a maze of passages.

Some appeared to be merely dead ends; others led to small bare rooms with panelled walls and mullioned windows, through which they could see and hear the blizzard still raging.

'I don't know how you find your way.' Anna's voice sounded small and lost in the hovering blackness.

'My sisters and I used to play here as children.'

Their footsteps echoing hollowly, they climbed an old oak staircase and went through an archway into a panelled antechamber.

Beyond were several bedrooms that, doors standing wide, led one into another. As Gideon lighted their way through them, Anna glimpsed huge four-posters with rich brocade hangings, many in tatters, and heavy sixteenth-century furniture.

The last room gave on to what appeared to be a long internal gallery panelled in dark wood from floor to ceiling.

Unlike the other panelling she'd seen, the lower half was heavily carved with flowers and fruit and trailing vines, while at intervals along the upper part were metal sconces.

Though the gallery had no windows, she could still hear the muffled moaning and whistling of the wind.

'Now we come to the really interesting bit,' Gideon said softly.

A quick glance at his face told her that this was the whole purpose of the little expedition.

His next words proved it.

'This is the haunted gallery and Sir Roger's domain,' Gideon told her in sepulchral tones. 'It's where he met his gruesome end, and where he still appears.'

'How did he meet his end?' The instant the words were out Anna wished she'd saved the question until they were safely back in the kitchen.

Not that she was scared. She didn't believe in ghosts. It was just that the hovering darkness, the all-pervading chill and the flickering candle made the atmosphere decidedly eerie.

'Before I tell you that,' Gideon said, 'I'd better provide a spot of background.'

Something about his manner, the way his eyes gleamed in the candlelight, was anything but reassuring.

She swallowed hard and waited.

'During the Civil War,' he began, 'Henry Strange, the then owner of Hartington Manor, while pretending to support the Roundheads, was in secret a Royalist. Henry's cousin, Sir Roger Strange, was an acknowledged Royalist and, late one snowy Christmas Eve, wounded, and with his enemies hard on his heels, he took refuge at the Manor. Because of the tell-tale tracks in the snow, a servant was dispatched to ride Sir Roger's horse well away from the house. Unfortunately the subterfuge failed, and in the middle of the night Cromwell's men banged on the door and demanded entry.

'Before he went down to let them in, Henry told his young wife Anne to hide Sir Roger until they'd gone. So, carrying a candle, Anne led him along this gallery and hid him in a small space behind the heavy panelling, promising to come and let him out as soon as the coast was clear. But after a fruitless search of the house, the Roundheads imprisoned Henry and set up temporary headquarters here. Afraid for her husband's life, and under strict surveillance, Anne could do nothing. It was over a month before they finally left...'

'You mean the poor man just stayed shut in there until he died of starvation?'

'More likely of thirst or loss of blood,' Gideon said practically.

Anna shuddered. 'How awful. And you say he still appears?'

'Only under certain circumstances.'

There was a strange note in his voice and, a faint suspicion forming at the back of her mind, Anna said, 'You mean if it's Christmas Eve?'

'There's rather more to it than that, and tonight the circumstances are just right.

'You see, the story goes that if a young woman walks alone down the gallery on a snowy Christmas Eve, carrying a lighted candle and without looking back, when she reaches the place where he was entombed, Sir Roger will appear.'

The suspicion strengthening, Anna muttered, 'I bet!' Then, crisply, 'Tell me something—Henry's wife, Anne, was she about my height and build, with dark hair and grey eyes?'

'How did you guess?'

'Call it second sight.'

'You think I'm having you on?'

'I'm sure of it,' Anna said with great conviction. 'In any case, I don't believe in ghosts.'

'If that's so, what are you scared of?'

'I'm not scared.'

'So why not put it to the test? All you have to do is take the candle and walk to the end of the gallery while I wait here... I remember my younger sister doing it when she was about eleven.'

'Then you *haven't* made the whole thing up?'

'Certainly not. I may have embroidered the tale a little,' he admitted with a grin, 'but it's well chronicled in the family archives. So if you want a chance to see ''a real live ghost''...'

'I'm not sure I do.'

'Go on,' he urged, 'give it a whirl.'

As she hesitated, he asked mockingly, 'Where's your sense of adventure?'

For some strange reason it had temporarily deserted her but, unwilling to admit that, she objected weakly, 'It all seems a bit silly.'

'Oh, well, if you really haven't got the courage...'

Far from willing to let him think she was an abject coward—though why should it matter *what* he thought of her?—Anna took a deep breath and agreed, 'All right, give me the candle.'

Handing her the iron candlestick, he asked, 'Sure you've got the nerve to go through with it?'

'If you've got the nerve to wait here in the dark?'

'Touché.' He gave her a mocking salute. 'Don't forget you're not supposed to look back.'

Telling herself stoutly that the whole thing was just a silly game, something to be played on Christmas Eve, like Murder or Charades, Anna began to walk down the gallery.

From behind her came a faint scraping sound, as though Gideon had drawn his foot along the black oak floorboards.

Her head held high, she made herself walk slowly. The flickering candlelight pushed back a Stygian blackness that retreated reluctantly before her and closed in triumphantly again behind her.

The urge to turn and look back, became overwhelming and she threw a quick glance over her shoulder. There was nothing visible within the pool of radiance cast by the candlelight. Letting out a relieved breath, she kept walking.

She was almost at the end of the gallery when, without any warning, there was a gust of icy air and the candle went out.

As she stood rooted to the spot, a cold hand reached out of the darkness and took hers.

The sudden shock made her heart miss a beat and stopped her breath. The candlestick fell from her nerveless fingers, hit the floor with a thud, and rolled away.

For a second or two her entire body remained frozen, but then her brain began to work with a sudden sharp clarity.

Taking a deep breath, she said furiously, 'Damn you to hell, Gideon Strange! You frightened me half to death.'

She heard his soft, satisfied chuckle in the darkness, then his voice, saying, 'You seemed so wary, I thought you must be half expecting it.'

'Well, I wasn't,' she told him shortly. Adding, 'I'm just glad I don't suffer from a weak heart.'

'In that case, so am I,' he said in a heartfelt voice. 'Much as I—' he broke off abruptly. Then went on, 'Much as I like a joke, I wouldn't care to have your death on my conscience.'

She got the distinct impression that it wasn't what he'd started to say.

The cold draught that had extinguished the candle continued to blow and, teeth chattering, she said, 'If I don't get warm soon, you may still have.'

When he said nothing, she added tartly, 'So, now you've had your little joke, do you think we could go back?'

'Certainly.' His voice sounded cool and contained. 'I dare say that at a pinch I could find my way back in the dark, but it might make more sense to locate the candle.'

He let go of her hand, and after a moment she heard him feeling around the floor.

'Ah! here it is.' A moment later a matchbox rattled, a match scraped, and the candle flared into life. He was holding it at waist height, and his face, lit from below, momentarily took on the grotesque qualities of a Hallowe'en mask.

As he shielded the flickering flame, she noticed a black hole in the dark panelling behind him, and realised that it was the source of the draught.

'Better close this up,' he remarked casually and, holding the candle to one side, reached to press the centre of a carved rose.

With scarcely a sound, the open panel slid into place, cutting off the flow of air.

'Now the fire calls, and the quickest way back is through

this door…' He turned, and the candle illuminated the end wall of the gallery.

Anna had thought it was a dead end, but let into the dark wainscoting was a small door she'd failed to notice. Though in the circumstances that wasn't surprising, she thought trenchantly.

'If you'd like to hold my hand?' Gideon suggested.

Though she could detect no sign of mockery in the offer, she answered briefly, 'Thank you, but no.'

'Then stay close. There's a spiral staircase with crumbling steps that are awkward to negotiate even in a good light…'

By the time they reached the blessed warmth of the kitchen, a combination of cold and the after-effects of the shock she'd suffered had started to take their toll and, despite all her efforts, she was trembling in every limb.

Gideon helped her off with her coat and, feeling the tremors running through her, steered her over to the fire and pushed her into a chair.

Annoyed by what she saw as her own weakness, she managed, 'I'm sorry.' Her voice shook.

He piled on more logs, and, watching her stretch her feet towards the blaze, asked, 'Feet cold?'

She nodded.

'Then let's have these off.' Stooping, he pulled off her thin suede boots and stood them to one side.

'Thank you.' Then with an attempt at humour, 'And, after all that, I still haven't managed to see a ghost.'

Gazing down at her pale face, he said abruptly, 'You look like a ghost yourself.'

He moved away, only to return after a moment with a glass of brandy. 'I'll make some coffee, but in the meantime drink this.'

'I don't like brandy,' she protested.

'You don't have to like it. This is for medicinal purposes.' Standing over her, he insisted, 'Go on, take a drink. It's good for shock.'

She lifted it to her lips, but her hand shook so much that the glass chinked against her teeth and she was forced to use both slender hands to hold it steady while she sipped.

The fiery liquid trickling down her throat made her cough, but almost immediately its warming effects began to brace her.

Watching as a little colour returned to her cheeks, he said, 'That's better. Now finish it up while I get the coffee.'

Shuddering from time to time, she drank obediently while she stared into the fire and thought about what had happened.

Although Gideon had *meant* to frighten her, she couldn't credit that it had just been done for a joke, as he'd tried to make her believe.

Without really knowing him, she felt convinced he wasn't that kind of man. Whatever his motives, they stemmed from something a good deal more serious.

Anger? Hatred? A desire for vengeance?

All very dramatic and quite ridiculous, she told herself crossly. They'd only just met and, though she had been the unintentional cause of his accident, he surely didn't hold that against her...?

'Here we are.' Gideon put the tray of coffee on the stool. 'A little cream, no sugar?'

'Please.'

Having poured the coffee and handed her a cup, he splashed more brandy into her glass, before helping himself to a small amount and taking a seat opposite.

His eyes on her now slightly flushed face, he remarked, 'You were looking very thoughtful.'

The coffee was good and hot and very welcome, and she took several sips before answering, 'I was wondering why you'd felt it necessary to frighten me.'

Regarding her shrewdly, he asked, 'You don't believe it was just a practical joke?'

'No,' she said baldly. 'I think you could be ruthless, if you felt it necessary, but I hadn't put you down as being either thoughtless or deliberately unkind.'

His lips tightened a little, as if the shot had gone home.

Then, as though still not totally convinced, he pursued, 'And you say you had no idea what might be going to happen?'

It was plain that he'd expected her to know, or at least guess what kind of game they were playing.

'No idea at all.'

She couldn't tell from his closed expression whether or not he believed her.

'I knew you were trying to scare me, of course, but I thought that all it involved was the walk along the gallery...' Grimacing, she went on, 'When the candle blew out and you took hold of my hand, I nearly died.'

'That was something I hadn't planned,' he admitted. 'All I'd intended to do was wait until you drew level and then step out. When we were plunged into total darkness, I merely took advantage of it.'

Her hair had come loose, and, pushing back a dark silky strand, she said, 'As soon as I saw the opening, I realised there must be a secret passage, but I still can't fathom where the draught came from.'

'For added security, both ends of the passage lead outside. Though the exits have bars across now, neither are sealed, so there's always a current of air funnelled through it. But this time I hadn't taken into account the strength of the wind.'

No wonder they had been able to hear that muffled moaning and whistling...

Thinking back to those few nerve-racking minutes in the gallery, she said, 'There's something else I don't understand. When I walked away, you were left in the dark, so how could you see to open panels and find your way through the passage?'

'I had a pencil torch in my pocket,' he admitted.

'But if you had a *torch*, why take a candle? No, silly question,' she added, a shade bitterly.

His face unreadable, he told her, 'Believe me, I wouldn't have tried to frighten you like that if I hadn't thought you'd be at least partly prepared.'

'Why should I have been prepared?'

After a brief pause, he answered, 'Well, earlier I'd mentioned sliding panels and a secret passage...'

Yes, that was quite true—he had. Yet somehow it hardly seemed enough.

'And, in order to get ahead of you, I was forced to open the first panel before you'd gone very far. It made a scraping noise and I felt sure you must have heard it.'

'I did, though at that minute I didn't realise what it was. If I had, I might have put two and two together.'

'If you didn't put two and two together, all I can say is you were very cool about the whole thing. A lot of women would have had screaming hysterics.'

Glancing up, she saw that his hard face held a touch of respect, possibly even admiration.

His approval was strangely sweet. But, incurably honest, she said, 'I'm afraid you can't put it down to bravery. For the first few seconds I was completely frozen, then, when I realised who it was holding my hand, I was too angry to be frightened.'

'How did you identify me so quickly?'

'I couldn't imagine a ghost wearing a signet-ring,' she said drily, 'but I knew *you* did. I'd noticed it earlier.'

'Ah!' he said softly. Then, reaching for the cafétière, 'Ready for some more coffee?'

'Please.'

He refilled her cup and, without consulting her, poured more brandy for them both.

For a while, as the logs crackled and blazed merrily and the snow beat against the windows, she sipped in silence.

At first she'd found it difficult to drink the strong, fiery spirit, but the more she drank, the easier it became.

When she glanced up, Gideon was watching her with a brooding look. A look that totally unnerved her.

A second later it was gone, replaced by what she was starting to recognise as his normal, slightly ironic expression.

Reaching over, he took her hand and, his voice holding a touch of wry self-mockery, asked, 'If I give you my abject apologies for what I did, is there any chance of being forgiven?'

Her composure shattered by the way he was holding her hand, and the gentle pressure of his thumb stroking her palm, she stammered, 'Y-yes, of course. Though you don't need to apologise. There was no real harm done.'

His long, heavy-lidded eyes smiled into hers, and she saw flecks of gold dancing in their green depths. Softly, he said, 'In the circumstances, that's very generous of you.'

He was still holding her hand and, becoming aware that she was gazing at him like a mesmerised rabbit, she hastily withdrew it.

Rushing into speech to try and hide her reaction to his overwhelming attraction, she asked, 'So the story about the ghost and how Sir Roger met his death was all made up?'

Regarding her with considerable amusement, the cause of which she preferred not to speculate on, he answered, 'It most definitely was not. Though I have my doubts about the ghost bit, the actual facts are well documented.'

'But if there was a secret passage that led outside, why didn't he go through it?'

'There is *now*, but there certainly wasn't *then*. Some time

after Sir Roger's tragic end, and presumably to prevent anything like that ever happening again, it seems that Henry
had the passage constructed. There's a story to the effect
that, after it was completed, the men who'd worked on it
were quietly done away with, so none of them could di-
vulge the secret to anyone else.'

Seeing her expression, he shrugged slightly. 'They were
pretty ruthless in those days.'

After a moment, she remarked, 'If the story's true, and
there really are such things as ghosts, I'd expect Sir Roger
to have company.'

Gideon's white, healthy teeth gleamed as he laughed.
'You have a point there. So it's just as well we have plenty
of room.'

She found herself staring at his mouth. It was the kind
of mouth that made butterflies flutter in her stomach and
sent little shivers running down her spine. The kind of
mouth that made her wish...

Realising he was watching her from beneath those long,
thick lashes, she hastily looked away.

Before she could think of anything to say, the lights went
out again.

This time they stayed out.

'It appears that the generator has packed up completely,'
Gideon observed. 'I'll have to have another look at it in
the morning.'

'Can't you look at it now?' Anna asked anxiously.

Firelight flickered on his face and gleamed in his eyes.
'It's housed in the old coach-house which now serves as a
garage and, apart from the fact that it's bound to be freezing
out there, mending a generator is a two-handed job.'

All at once, the vague realisation that had been hovering
on the periphery of her mind crystallised into a certainty.

'Don't try to tell me your arm won't work,' she said

crisply. 'You've been using two hands since you picked up the candlestick in the gallery.'

'That's quite true,' he admitted mildly. 'The use gradually returned, as I felt sure it would.'

'So you have *two* hands to mend the generator,' she pressed.

'Well, as there's no lighting, I'd need one to hold the torch.'

It all sounded logical enough, yet she found herself wondering if he was looking for an excuse *not* to mend the generator.

'I'll hold the torch for you.'

He shook his head. 'I won't hear of you going out there and getting frozen again, after all you've been through. In any case, I doubt if I could lay hands on a torch, so it makes sense to wait until daylight.'

'You told me you *had* a torch,' she said accusingly.

'I'm afraid that one would be nowhere near powerful enough. It has only a narrow spotlight beam that's useful in confined spaces but not for much else.'

He seemed to have an answer for everything.

'There's no need to look so concerned,' he added lightly. 'What could be more romantic than going to bed by candlelight?'

He seemed almost pleased at the prospect, Anna thought vexedly, as if, for some reason, candlelight suited his purpose.

CHAPTER FOUR

WELL aware of her agitation, he asked innocently, 'Don't you agree it's romantic?'

'The word I had in mind was "inconvenient",' she told him shortly.

He sighed. 'Isn't it funny how the withdrawal of the modern amenities everyone takes for granted throws people into a panic?'

'I am *not* in a panic.' Too late she realised he was baiting her, and bit her lip.

'The thing that is inconvenient,' he pursued, 'is the lack of central heating. The bedrooms are anything but warm.'

'Are there no fireplaces?'

'Unfortunately my father had most of the chimneys boarded up. Though I believe a fire can be lit in the master bedroom.'

He rose to his feet and stretched leisurely. 'I'll go and check, and while I'm at it I'll take your case up.'

When he'd gone, warm and comfortable now, her head resting against the back of the chair, her eyelids drooping, Anna sat and stared into the flames.

Half-asleep and half-awake, she listened idly to the blizzard still raging outside, while thoughts drifted in and out of her mind.

This wasn't at all how she'd visualised herself spending Christmas Eve. But since the break-up with David, and her return to Rymington, nothing had gone according to plan.

As far as her business life was concerned, she had failed dismally. The same with her private life.

Nursing her hurt, her sense of betrayal, she had avoided

making any new relationships, and gone back to freezing off any man who had tried to come too close.

But over the past few months she'd thought about David a great deal less, and in consequence had gone a long way towards regaining her equilibrium...

Only to meet Gideon Strange and be rocked afresh by that elusive likeness, and the power of his attraction.

Unlike David, he had strength and depth and maturity, and though his mouth showed a disturbing sensuality, that sensuality was balanced by an austere self-control.

Though she scarcely knew him, she knew with a sure and certain instinct that he was everything she had *thought* David was.

She closed her eyes with a sigh. It was as though fate was playing some kind of game with her. A game she stood little chance of winning...

Something made her stir and open her eyes.

Gideon was standing gazing down at her. There was a look on his face that made her heart start to race with a swift urgency. A look that, innocent as she was, she couldn't fail to recognise. A look of naked desire.

The following second his expression showed nothing but faint amusement.

Had that look of desire been only a trick of the flickering light? Or, just waking from a doze, had she dreamt it?

No, fleeting though it had been, she was certain she'd neither dreamt it nor imagined it.

'I—I think I must have dropped off,' she stammered.

'Does that mean you're ready for bed?'

'No!' She was remembering that look, and her voice was shrill with panic. Endeavouring to take a grip on herself, she peered at her watch. 'It's only a quarter to eleven. That's far too early.'

'Well, if you don't want to go to bed, I'd better make sure we stay warm enough.'

He picked up a large iron poker and stirred the fire, making it crackle and blaze and sending a shower of bright sparks up the chimney, before throwing on a couple of fresh logs.

Resuming his seat, he asked, 'What time do you go as a rule?'

'Not before eleven,' she lied. 'And then I always take a book. In any case, this *is* Christmas Eve.'

'So are you planning to wait up for Santa Claus?'

'I used to want to as a child, but I was always sent to bed.'

'So you believed in him?'

'Oh, yes, until I was about six or seven. My mother used to leave a glass of brandy and a mince pie on the mantelpiece, and they were always gone by morning.'

Picking up his own glass, Gideon remarked, 'Speaking of brandy, you haven't finished yours.'

She had thought she had, or very nearly, and was surprised to see how much was left.

As she drank, he remarked, 'With no make-up on and your hair loose like that, you look about fifteen. How old are you now, Anna?'

'Twenty-four.'

'Tell me about yourself. Apart from the fact that you once believed in Santa Claus and now you're a qualified librarian—'

There it was again, that subtle mockery.

'—I know very little about you.'

'There's not much *to* know. I'm afraid I lead a very dull life.'

'No live-in lover to share your bedsit?'

'No. Which is just as well, as I've only got a single bed.'

Gideon grinned. 'Well, that in itself could lend a touch of excitement.'

'With a four feet by four feet bathroom, excitement would hardly be the word,' she commented drily.

'Oh I don't know!' He leered theatrically at her. 'I can think of worse things.'

'Such as being alone at Christmas?'

Ignoring the dig, he pursued, 'But if there's no live-in lover, you must have a boyfriend? Someone special, perhaps?'

Wishing he'd drop the subject, she said shortly, 'No.'

'How long have you been back in Rymington?'

'The best part of a year.'

He lifted a well-marked brow. 'Well, unless all the men are blind round here, there must be plenty of eager males only too willing to fill the role?'

There was certainly one. Though, being fairly staid and having just turned forty, Paul would hardly fit in the category of *boyfriend*.

'So *why* haven't you got a boyfriend?'

Goaded, she snapped, 'Because I don't happen to *want* one.'

'Ah...' Gideon murmured softly. 'Perhaps you see yourself as an elusive enchantress in a fairy story. Alluring and hauntingly beautiful. A woman every man wants, but who wants none of them...'

Made uncomfortable by the comparison, she objected, 'You make me sound cold and heartless.'

'And you're not?'

'No, I'm not!' she cried angrily.

Yet even while she denied it she remembered guiltily that some of the would-be lovers she had kept at bay throughout her college years had used those exact words.

But while most of her fellow students had been falling in love—or lust—and bemoaning the fact that the Hall of Residence cramped their style, no man had really turned her on.

Because of her looks, there had been plenty willing to try. With one or two she had dabbled in a little light romance—like someone cautiously testing the temperature of the bath water—until they had started to want more.

But all she had really looked for from any of them had been companionship, someone to share things with when Cleo had become totally wrapped up with the man who was to be her future husband.

'Now I've made you mad again,' Gideon observed without any apparent remorse. 'But it seems a little…shall we say *unusual* for a woman of twenty-four never to have had a boyfriend—'

'I didn't say I'd *never* had a boyfriend,' she broke in crossly. 'As a matter of fact, I've had quite a few.'

With smooth effrontery, he asked, 'And were you serious about any of them?'

'Mainly they were just friends,' she admitted. 'There was no one who meant anything to me until—'

She stopped abruptly. The last person she wanted to talk about was David.

But Gideon wasn't to be put off. 'Until someone special came along?' he suggested.

'Yes.'

'So tell me about this special man.'

When she stayed silent, he hazarded mockingly, 'I dare say he was tall, dark and handsome?'

'He was tall, *fair* and handsome,' she corrected.

'When I first got into your car, you looked quite shaken, and you remarked that I reminded you of someone you used to know. Was that *him* by any chance?'

'Yes,' she said tightly.

'So are we very much alike?'

'No, not really. It's just that at odd times I can see a fleeting resemblance.'

'What kind of man was he?'

'Charismatic, well educated, well spoken and utterly charming.'

'What did he do?'

'He worked for Drombies, a firm of auctioneers and valuers, but he hated it. He said he shouldn't have had to work.'

'Does that mean his family were wealthy?'

'Not that I know of. I got the impression his parents were dead. I don't think he had any other family. If he had, he never mentioned them.'

His face curiously devoid of expression, Gideon queried, 'Never?'

'No, never.'

'Didn't he ever tell you about his background? Or ask about yours?'

Puzzled by his persistence, she said, 'No. The nights we saw each other, we always went out. I suppose we didn't get much chance to talk, and when we did it was always about his plans for the future rather than about the past...'

Getting to his feet, Gideon stirred the logs. His broad back was to her, and she saw tension in his muscular neck and shoulders.

Returning to his seat after a moment, he asked, 'So what happened? Did you get tired of him?'

'No.'

He pursed his lips. 'I refuse to believe he got tired of you.'

Uncomfortably, she said, 'I'd rather not talk about it.'

She hadn't even told Cleo the full story, simply that she'd had a boyfriend and they'd split up.

'If by any chance you're still stuck on him,' Gideon remarked practically, 'it might help to talk about it, to get it out of your system.'

No, she wasn't still 'stuck on him'. Just knowing that

brought a feeling of release, of freedom, made her able to let go of the past.

But it was still something she didn't want to talk about.

Reading her reluctance, he pressed, 'How long had you known him? Was he a fellow student?'

'No. It was quite a while after I'd left college. I'd been working in London for almost eighteen months.'

'Then how and where did you meet him?'

'I met him in Sussex. The contents of a county mansion, including an extensive library, came up for auction, and I went to bid for some of the books.'

Perhaps it was the amount of brandy she'd drunk that loosened her tongue, or maybe, as Gideon had suggested, she needed to get it out of her system.

Whichever, she found herself embarking on the whole sorry tale.

'I was waiting for the sale to start when he came over to ask if I had a catalogue. We got talking, and he invited me to have a bite to eat with him at lunchtime. I said yes. Later, though he was supposed to be working, he managed to slip away and take me for a meal in the nearby town. He was pleased to find that, like himself, I lived in London, and he asked me to have dinner with him that same evening.'

'So you were, in effect, swept off your feet?' Gideon asked a touch cynically.

With a sigh, she agreed, 'You could say that. Less than a week later he told me that he loved me...'

And, believing him, she had walked on air.

'Go on,' Gideon prompted.

Her head felt light, as though it were floating, and she had to concentrate. 'He started to press me to sleep with him. He said it was the norm these days...'

'And did you?'

'No.'

His level brows shot up. 'Why not? Aren't you in favour of any grown woman having freedom of choice in matters of sex?'

'Yes, I am,' she said after a moment. 'But freedom of choice means being able to say *no* as well as yes.'

An expression she couldn't decipher flitted across Gideon's face before he asked, 'So sexually he didn't turn you on?'

'Yes, he did.'

'Then why did you hold back? Did he prove to be married or something?'

'No, he wasn't married. He was only twenty-two at the time, a year younger than I was, but he made no secret of the fact that since the age of fifteen there had been a string of women in his life, and sometimes more than one at a time. Which wasn't surprising, I suppose. He was very good-looking and had loads of sex appeal.'

'Presumably his previous girlfriends were all happy to jump into bed with him?'

'Apparently the one or two who weren't didn't last long. He described it as "wasting his time".'

'You make him sound like a shallow, selfish young swine,' Gideon observed coldly.

Though she hadn't really meant to, that was a fair summing up, Anna thought sadly, but it had taken her until now to see it. No wonder people said that love was blind.

'So what did you do?'

Sighing, she went on, 'I kept saying no. I didn't like the idea of casual sex. It wasn't what I wanted...'

'You were hoping for some kind of...shall we say, commitment?'

'Yes.' She tried not to yawn.

'And eventually he gave in and bought you an engagement ring?'

She shook her head, then wished she hadn't when the room began to whirl.

'He *didn't* buy you a ring?'

'No.'

'Did he say he was going to?'

'No.'

'But he led you to think he might?'

'Not even that. I can never say he wasn't honest. He told me straight that if it was marriage I was after, I'd fallen in love with the wrong man. He said something like, ''Men are naturally polygamous. The idea of tying myself to one woman for life fills me with horror. In my opinion, marriage is an outdated, outmoded, institution.'''

'But you didn't agree?'

'No.'

Unlike David, and perhaps because of the example set by her own loving parents, she had always believed in marriage, for better or worse, and a lifetime's fidelity to one man.

'What happened?'

She was forced to stifle a yawn before going on, 'He was infuriated by what he called my old-fashioned attitude, but he still wanted me...'

'So, instead of ditching you like the others, he kept trying to persuade you to change your mind?'

'Yes.'

'Did he succeed?'

'Yes and no.'

She saw Gideon's lips tighten before he said, 'You might need to explain that.'

Anna was finding it difficult to think clearly, and despite all her efforts her speech was becoming a little slurred as she went on, 'One Friday night, when we'd been to an early show and gone back to his flat for coffee, he made another attempt to persuade me to stay. When I refused, he said,

"Look, you know I'm mad about you and, just to prove there's nothing *casual* about all this, I'm asking you to move in with me.'''

She had *wanted* to, but, a woman at war with her own standards, she had still hesitated.

'When I didn't immediately say yes, he promised, "If you're worried about other women, I give you my word that you are the only woman in my life and will be from now on." He sounded as though he meant it, and I thought he might have changed...'

'But you didn't seriously expect someone like David to change?'

Stifling yet another yawn, she asked thickly, 'How do you know his name was David?'

'You must have mentioned it.'

She couldn't *remember* mentioning David by name, but she must have done. No doubt the unaccustomed alcohol, as well as encouraging her to talk, had made her just a little bit woozy.

A log flared and sputtered briefly, then broke, settling into white ash. In the hall, the grandfather clock began to chime midnight.

Watching her eyelids start to droop, Gideon rose to his feet, remarking, 'I think it's high time we went to bed before you fall sound asleep in your chair.'

She looked at him owlishly. 'I was waiting up for Santa Claus.'

'Didn't your mother ever tell you that he won't come while you *are* up? But if you go to bed like a good girl you may hear his sleigh-bells.'

He brought the candle and lit it from the fire before asking, 'About ready?'

Having struggled to her feet, she swayed, lost her balance, and sat down again abruptly.

'Dear me,' he said with a touch of wry amusement, 'it

seems we've overdone the brandy. Oh, well, I'm sure we'll manage.'

Blowing out the candle, he put it on the table and, stooping, scooped her out of the chair and into his arms.

The flickering fire lit their way across to the door, and he used an elbow to press the handle. Once in the hall, the high mullioned windows let in enough snowy light to mitigate the darkness and make climbing the stairs relatively easy.

Through the leaded panes, Anna could vaguely see that the blizzard was still blowing. Snow had piled up on the sills in white drifts, while a myriad snowflakes went swirling past.

Gideon's prediction that they would be snowed up by the morning looked as if it would come true, yet somehow the thought had ceased to alarm her.

Her head felt light, buoyant and floating. The sensation, in itself a quite pleasant one, was accompanied by a feeling of unreality.

Peering into the face so close to hers, she said accusingly, 'We should have had a candle, you know.'

Walking along the wide landing, Gideon asked, 'Don't you think we're managing quite well without one?'

'You said going to bed by candlelight would be romantic.'

He glanced down at her, and she saw the glimmer of his teeth as he smiled. 'Don't you think being carried to bed is equally romantic?'

'It only happens in stories.'

'It's happening now.'

'But this isn't *real*, is it?'

'Well, I'll tell you what, so you won't be disappointed, I'll light the candles in the bedroom.'

'Yes, that would be nice,' she said solemnly.

Along the wide passage it was darker, but still he moved

unerringly. Part-way along, he stooped a little to open the door into a large bedroom, then used his foot to close it again behind them.

In the wide stone grate a goodly pile of logs burnt and flickered, lighting the room and gleaming on the old polished furniture. Though the fire had taken the chill off the air, it was still far from warm.

Gideon put her down in a high-backed cushioned chair close to the hearth, and proceeded to light a pair of three-branched candelabra.

Raising a quizzical brow, he asked, 'Happy, now?'

'Yes, thank you,' she said politely.

'I'd better put one of these in your bathroom, so you can see to clean your teeth.'

'Have I got a bathroom?'

'This is the master suite, so there's one at each end. A his and hers.'

For some reason this struck her as funny, and she giggled. She felt happy, almost euphoric.

'You'd better have the nearest one.'

Opening a door to the left, he carried in one of the candelabra, and returned to ask, 'If I find your night things for you, do you think you can manage on your own?'

'Of course I can manage,' she said indignantly. 'Anyone would think I was drunk.'

'Anyone might be right.'

Of course she wasn't drunk. She didn't drink. But she was so tired that it seemed too much trouble to argue.

Her case was waiting on an oak chest, and, trying to stifle her yawns, she watched as he unzipped it and took out her nightdress, towelling robe and toilet bag.

When they had been transferred to the bathroom, he helped her up and, an arm around her waist, steered her through the open door.

Swaying slightly on her stockinged feet, she held on to the towel rail to steady herself.

'Sure you can manage?' he asked doubtfully.

'Abdholutely sure,' she said with dignity.

'Call me if you need me.' He went out, leaving the door slightly ajar.

Leaning against the sink, she cleaned her teeth and washed her face and hands.

A hot shower would have been nice, she thought wistfully, only the water was cold. But perhaps she was too tired to bother anyway...

The candles, placed on a shelf behind her, were reflected in the mirror, and her own face, pale and ghost-like, swam hazily in front of her.

Needing to steady herself frequently, and sit on the stool whenever possible, she fumbled out of her clothes and tights, shivering as the chilly air wrapped around her naked body.

It was somewhat easier to pull on her nightdress and robe.

That accomplished, she thought longingly of bed. Well, she would go, she decided, as soon as the floor stopped tilting.

There was a light rap, and Gideon's voice queried, 'About ready for bed?'

'Yes.'

Pushing open the door, he suggested, 'Then you'd better let me give you a hand.'

He was wearing a burgundy silk dressing-gown that came to his knees. His legs and feet were bare.

Blinking at him, she asked, 'Are you going to bed, too?'

Picking her up in his arms and walking through to the bedroom, he answered, 'Yes.'

'Where are you sleeping?'

'I thought I'd share this room. That way we can keep each other warm.'

Nestling against him, she agreed, 'Yes, please, I'd like that.'

Anna stirred, and began to surface slowly. For a while she lay half-asleep and half-awake, while the mists gradually cleared and thoughts and questions began to filter into her consciousness.

This didn't feel at all like her own, rather hard bed-settee. The mattress was a great deal more comfortable, the pillows were softer, and the duvet was feather-light, but warm. So where was she?

After a short struggle her befuddled brain produced the answer. It was Christmas, and she must be at Cleo's.

But she hadn't a clue how she'd spent the evening, nor could she remember changing into her night things and going to bed.

She couldn't even recall drinking Cleo's home-made punch, as she had the previous year. Though, judging by her throbbing head, she must have done. She never normally got headaches, but the innocent-tasting punch had a kick like a mule.

Trying to think back, the only thing she could clearly recall was leaving the shop. It had been snowing, and everywhere was white-over. The cobbles had been slippy, and she had walked through to the car park with care...

Having got so far, memory pressed *play*, and what followed went through her mind as though she were watching a video.

The accident... Seeing Gideon Strange for the first time... Driving him home... The blizzard... His offer of a job... Her car refusing to start... The disturbing evening they had spent together... How he'd pressed her to tell him about David...

Then what?

But the video stopped there and stubbornly refused to give her any more. She couldn't remember what had happened after that, or how she had got to bed.

The only other thing she could recall, the thing she had tried to *avoid* recalling, was the attraction that had flared between them...

No, not *between* them. It had all been on her side. His smooth abrasiveness, his calculated mockery, his attempt to scare her, all went to prove that he felt nothing for her.

Yet for reasons of his own, reasons she failed to understand, he *wanted* her to stay.

And she was torn.

Common sense—or was it simply self-preservation?—insisted she should go as soon as possible, while that powerful fascination she felt tempted her to throw caution to the winds and stay.

But she knew in her heart of hearts that it would be both foolish and dangerous to remain here. If she let this fascination take over, she would end up badly hurt. He didn't want her...

No, that wasn't so. He *did* want her; she could instinctively sense it. But if there *was* an attraction on his side, it was a reluctant one.

She stiffened her resolve to leave, that morning. In fact, straight after breakfast...

But how was she to leave if her car wouldn't start? And she couldn't phone for a taxi—even supposing any taxi firm was working on Christmas Day. That only left walking back to town.

Oh, well. Needs must when the devil drives. Though it would depend very much on how bad the conditions were. If it had continued to snow all night...

Opening her eyes to an almost blinding brilliance, Anna

promptly closed them again, and put a hand to her aching head.

One thing was certain: she couldn't blame Cleo's punch for her headache. It must be due to the amount of brandy she'd drunk.

After a second or two she cautiously opened her eyes once more, to find that the room was full of snow-reflected light and sunshine. Even the fire burning brightly in the grate was diminished by it.

Through the mullioned windows on her right she could see that the blizzard had blown itself out and the sky was clear and blue.

Pushing herself up against the pillows, she peered out. Snow covered everything, making wind-blown dunes on the window-sills, half burying the shrubs and bushes, stippling the tree trunks and weighing down the green arms of the pine.

Taking into account the amount of snow that had fallen, the length of the drive up to the Manor, and the fact that because Old Castle Road wound along a ridge it frequently became impassable in snowy weather, Anna didn't give much for her chances of getting away just yet.

It seemed she might have to spend Christmas Day with Gideon Strange, whether she wanted to or not...

Unless there was a sudden and dramatic thaw, she thought, clutching at straws. The sun was bright enough... It was also high in the sky, she realised. So what time was it?

As she turned her head to glance at her watch, her eyes were drawn to the space beside her and she froze, sitting like a statue while it sank in that though she was alone in the king-sized bed *now*, someone else had undoubtedly slept there.

Knocked completely off balance, she fought against the

knowledge, but the pillow to her left bore the unmistakable imprint of another head...

As though the shock had triggered some release mechanism, Anna's recollection of the previous night—which had stopped with her talking about David—began to unfold in another series of pictures.

Though they were foggy and indistinct, she could see herself being carried up the stairs. Sitting by the fire. Being helped into the bathroom. Then Gideon asking if she was ready for bed...

Though she could go no further than that, the rest was self-evident.

While she struggled to come to terms with this new and shattering knowledge, there was a tap, the bedroom door opened, and Gideon walked in carrying a large copper kettle.

He was wearing dark trousers and a fine black polonecked sweater. His jaw was freshly shaven, and his corn-coloured hair looked damp.

'Good morning,' he said cheerfully, putting the kettle on the hearth. 'Or perhaps, as it's gone twelve, I should say good afternoon.'

Taking a couple of logs from the large basket that stood to one side, he built up the fire before coming to stand by the bed and look down at her.

With her demure cotton nightie, and her dark hair tumbled around her shoulders, she looked absurdly young and innocent, he thought.

Stiffly, she turned her head and looked up at him.

Noting her white, stricken face, he queried, 'Something wrong?'

'You slept in my bed.'

'No, *you* slept in *my* bed.'

'Y-you *bastard*,' she said shakily.

He clicked his tongue reprovingly. 'That's not a nice word for a well brought-up young lady to use.'

'It might not be *nice* but it's *justified*. Though you knew how I felt about casual sex, you deliberately set out to seduce me...'

CHAPTER FIVE

'How very melodramatic,' he mocked, making no attempt to deny the accusation.

'You gave me brandy, when I wasn't used to it,' she choked, 'and then took advantage of me.'

His face amused, he told her, 'That sounds just like a line from some Victorian novel.'

'How can you stand there and laugh when you know it's true?' she asked bitterly.

He shook his head. 'I plead guilty to the first half of the charge, but not the second.'

'Don't try and deny you slept in the same bed.'

'I won't. But that doesn't mean I took advantage of you. Or even that I *intended* to.'

'Why else would you have done it?'

'Because it was the sensible option. The rest of the bedrooms are like ice-boxes. Even this room got cold in the early morning, as I knew it would when the fire died down. But, sleeping together, we kept each other warm. Nothing more, nothing less.'

Though she badly wanted to believe him, remembering that look of naked desire she'd seen on his face earlier in the evening, she couldn't. 'You're lying!' she cried hoarsely.

'I can assure you that, apart from carrying you to bed and tucking you in, I never laid a finger on you.'

With a reminiscent smile, he added, 'Though I must say you were in a very receptive mood—'

'I don't believe you,' she choked.

'It's the truth.'

Flushing painfully, she said, 'I'd had far too much to drink.'

Then, accusingly, 'If you weren't planning to seduce me, why did you give me so much?' Guessing what he was going to say, she added sharply, 'And don't tell me it was just for medicinal purposes.'

'You were very uptight. You'd been that way all evening. A little alcohol is useful for loosening things up.'

'You mean doing away with inhibitions?'

Sounding completely unrepentant, he agreed, 'It certainly helps. But it seems you really weren't used to drinking...'

Suddenly uneasy, wondering just what she had said or done, she demanded, 'What exactly did you mean by a "receptive" mood?'

'You asked where I was sleeping, and when I said I thought I'd share this room so we could keep each other warm, you snuggled up to me and said, "Yes, please, I'd like that."'

'I didn't!'

'You most certainly did.'

As she gaped at him, aghast, he said with a twisted grin, 'I can't say what might have happened if you'd stayed awake, but you went out like a light.'

'Which made everything only too easy for you.'

A white line appearing round his mouth, he told her tightly, 'I don't get my kicks making love to unconscious women. I like my partners to be wide awake, and responsive.'

'I'm sorry,' she whispered after a moment. 'I shouldn't have said that. It was unforgivable.'

When he showed no sign of being appeased, she stammered, 'I—I didn't really mean it, truly I didn't.' Pressing waxy fingers to her throbbing temples, she repeated, 'I'm sorry...'

Suddenly it was all too much. Biting her lip, she stared down at the maroon and cream duvet.

He sat on the edge of the bed and a warm hand lifted her chin. When he saw her brimming eyes, his hard face softened.

'Don't worry about it…'

Even through her distress she was aware that he smelled fresh and clean and wholesome.

'And don't cry, whatever you do! Otherwise I might have to kiss you better.'

Taking a deep breath, she observed shakily, 'That sounds like a threat.'

'It was meant to.' Studying her pale face, the faint shadows beneath her eyes, he queried, 'Headache?'

'Yes.'

'I'll find you something for it. Now, would you prefer to have brunch in bed, or in front of the kitchen fire?'

Trying hard not to blink, in case the tears escaped, she said, 'In front of the kitchen fire.'

It seemed he never missed a thing. Taking a spotless hankie from his trouser pocket, he put it in her hand. 'This might come in handy.'

'Thank you.' She pressed it to her eyes and blew her nose.

'I wouldn't recommend a shower,' he went on drily. 'The water's glacial. But there's hot water in the kettle, so at least you can have a warm wash.'

'Sounds like heaven.'

'Would you like a cup of tea or coffee first?'

'I'd love a cup of tea.'

'There's a pot already made, so if you stay where you are for a moment I'll fetch you one.'

The mattress moved as his weight lifted from it.

Sitting motionless, she watched his broad back disappear through the door.

She was still trying to gather the remnants of her composure when he returned with a cup of tea and two white tablets, which he placed on the bedside table.

'These should take care of the headache. Now, while you sort yourself out I'll go and get on with the meal.' A twinkle in his eye, he added, 'When it's ready, I'll sound the gong.'

He was more than halfway across the room when she spoke his name. 'Gideon...'

His hand on the latch, he turned to look at her.

'Thank you.'

They both knew she was thanking him for a great deal more than a cup of tea.

He smiled at her, and his face held genuine warmth. A moment later the door closed softly behind him.

Still feeling shaken, Anna sat where she was while she swallowed the tablets and drank her tea. For the first time in her life she had shared a bed with a man. It was, as Cleo had once joked, a momentous occasion.

Only she couldn't recall any of it.

Which was just as well, she reminded herself sternly. If she hadn't 'gone out like a light', things might have ended differently.

Though he hadn't exactly admitted it, there was no doubt in her mind that Gideon had *planned* to seduce her, and had she stayed awake, her inhibitions lowered by alcohol, he would have found it all too easy.

Her face grew hot as she recalled him saying, 'When I said I thought I'd share this room so we could keep each other warm, you snuggled up to me and said, "Yes, please, I'd like that."'

Though she didn't want to believe it, it had the unmistakable ring of truth.

In vino veritas.

Thank the Lord she *had* flaked out. It had proved to be

the best defence, not only against him, but against her own weakness. Because she did want him. She had wanted him from the moment she saw him. It had been love at first sight…

Oh, don't be an idiot, she berated herself. Of course she didn't *love* him. Call what she felt for Gideon Strange fascination, infatuation, physical attraction, straightforward lust—*anything* rather than love.

Though being in love was what it felt like.

She had thought herself in love only once before, and what she'd felt then for David had been just a pale imitation of what she felt now.

The one real similarity they shared was that the men involved, though both charming, had only wanted to use her. It seemed that in the love stakes she was fated to be a loser.

Last night had proved to be a close call; she had been extremely lucky to keep what remained of her self-respect.

Though the decision brought a feeling of cold desolation, she determined that, once she had left the Manor, she would take care to steer well clear of any further involvement with its master.

But, for the moment at least, she was unable to leave. There was still a few precious hours that Fate had pressed on her to spend with Gideon.

It was the only time they would ever have together so, instead of regretting it, she would make the most of it. Enjoy it to the full.

Pushing back the duvet, she got out of bed, and donning her towelling robe, which lay over a chair, opened the nearest door and peered in.

In the oyster-tiled bathroom a tangy smell of shower-gel hung on the air, and spots of water still clung to the frosted glass of the shower-stall.

A man's toilet bag sat in a recess above the sink, next

to a battery-operated razor and a bottle of aftershave. The air was cold.

There was no sign of her own toilet bag, and vaguely she recalled Gideon saying something about two bathrooms.

Crossing the room, she found a second luxurious bathroom tiled in pearly-pink. Thankfully the door had been left ajar, and some warmth had seeped in.

Her clothes were in a little pile on the floor, and her toilet bag lay on a shelf next to a candelabra with burntout candles.

The water in the kettle was very hot, and half filled the sink. Feeling grateful to Gideon for thinking of it, she washed herself from head to toe and cleaned her teeth.

Standing in front of the fire, so that the heat toasted her legs, she donned clean undies, a pair of burgundy slacks, a fine wool shirt the colour of clotted cream, and her slippers.

She had just finished brushing her hair and knotting it loosely on top of her head, when she heard the resonant sound of a gong being struck.

Closing the bedroom door behind her, she trotted along the passage to the head of the stairs and, leaning over the oak balustrade, looked down into the hall, where Gideon was standing with a large, round-headed padded hammer in his hand.

'When you were in the States, did you ever work for J. Arthur Rank?' she enquired.

Head tipped back, he grinned up at her. 'I'm afraid they hadn't got a leopardskin my size.'

Her spirits rising for the first time in weeks, she made her way down to join him.

At the bottom of the stairs he took both her hands and said, 'Happy Christmas.'

Affected by his touch, his nearness, she echoed a trifle breathlessly, 'Happy Christmas.'

His eyes were fixed on her mouth. She watched his lips part and his head tilt a little, as if he intended to pull her close and kiss her.

Holding her breath, she waited. But after a moment he released her hands and turned away, adding mundanely, 'Everything's ready, so come and get it.'

After a tasty and satisfying meal, eaten in front of a blazing fire, Gideon stretched his long frame and announced, 'Now we need a spot of exercise.'

Warm and comfortable, and feeling distinctly idle, Anna looked at him with a 'you speak for yourself' expression.

He raised an eyebrow at her. 'Woman, we can't spend the whole of Christmas Day in idle sloth. There are things to do.'

'Such as the generator to mend.'

Shaking his head, he told her, 'Hopeless, I'm afraid. Luckily the larder is like an ice-house, so the food won't go off.'

Ignoring the latter sentence, she asked, 'How do you know it's hopeless?'

'I had a look at it this morning, while you were still in bed, but I couldn't make out what was wrong with it.'

From his laid-back manner, she got the impression that he hadn't tried very hard.

But perhaps she was judging him too harshly? How many people would actually be able to mend a generator? She wouldn't know what a generator looked like if she fell over one...

'Now to work!' He broke briskly into her thoughts. 'We've holly to gather, some spruce boughs to cut, a proper Yule log to saw and bring in, and we'll need to dig up a Christmas tree. There's one about the right size growing at the edge of the coppice.'

'*We*? Isn't that sort of thing men's work?'

'I thought these days women wanted equality?'

'Well, of course I'd love to help,' she assured him hastily, 'but I'm afraid I left my lumberjack gear at home.'

Eyeing her suede boots, which were standing in the inglenook, he asked, 'Is that all you have with you?'

'Apart from a pair of court shoes and these.' Lifting her feet, she displayed her black velvet slippers.

Shaking his head, he demanded, 'How can someone who looks like a beautiful, smoky-eyed witch be so unprepared?'

'I'm afraid my crystal ball got fogged up. When I left home yesterday morning, I had no idea it was going to snow.'

'Then the first thing we need to do is get you properly kitted out. While I see what I can find in the garden-room, I expect you'd like another cup of coffee?'

'Well, at least *your* crystal ball seems to be in working order,' she commented approvingly, as he refilled her cup.

The coffee was still hot and fragrant and, after a second's hesitation, he refilled his own.

'I thought you were off to the garden-room?'

He grinned at her, making her heart miss a beat. 'What was Adam's excuse? The woman tempted me. But after this spot of indulgence it's all hands on deck,' he added severely.

'No slacking?'

'None.'

As soon as Gideon had swallowed his coffee he put down his cup and disappeared into the servants' quarters.

Wishing this easy camaraderie could last, Anna lingered over hers.

He was back quite quickly with a miscellaneous pile of outdoor things over one arm, and two pairs of wellington boots, all of which he spread out on the hearth.

'There's everything we need here. They'll just take a little while to warm up.'

As a faint steam began to rise from the various garments, he added, 'Both pairs of boots are the same size, and they'll be far too big for you, but there are plenty of thick woollen socks to pad them out. And now, as your special treat, I'll let you have first choice of colour.'

'The red socks,' she said firmly, 'and that pair of wellingtons. I've often thought I'd like to join the green wellie brigade.'

He laughed. 'Whatever turns you on.'

Some five minutes later, having donned waterproof overtrousers, an Aran sweater, a man's sheepskin jacket, a red knitted hat, a scarf and a pair of thick gloves, she clumped after Gideon who, apart from being bare-headed, was similarly attired.

The garden-room, obviously used for changing outdoor footwear and clothing, had a row of pegs alongside a wooden bench.

Tools were arranged in neat rows, and a series of shelves held an orderly array of vases, flowerpots, seed-trays, and so on. Several bags of potting compost, and a couple of deep terracotta planters stood on the floor.

'One of those will be ideal for the tree,' Gideon remarked. Then, indicating a massive log propped in one corner, he suggested, 'And if we use that, it'll save us sawing up a tree trunk.'

'Wouldn't you call that *slacking*?' she asked drily.

'Expedient. It looks nice and dry, so it'll burn well.'

'Sold.'

Surveying her cumbersome boots and the heavy jacket, with its over-long sleeves and too-wide shoulders, his expression openly amused, he queried, 'Are you going to have enough strength to move about in that lot?'

'Of course,' she said loftily. 'At the moment, I could stand in for Mighty Mouse.'

After a brief inspection, he shook his head. 'The shoulders are the right size, but your ears aren't big enough.'

He yanked the woollen hat she was wearing well down over them and, after gathering up a selection of tools, opened the door and led the way across a low-walled terrace.

Sun shone brightly from a cornflower-blue sky and the air was as cold and sparkling as iced champagne. The snow, which came almost to the top of her wellingtons, lay crisp and even, its virginal surface unmarked except for a few bird tracks.

'Don't forget there are three steps down to the garden,' Gideon warned.

The steps safely negotiated, she noticed a trail of footprints going to, and coming from, a high single-storey building on the left.

Judging from the design, it had once been a rather grand coach-house, but was now, presumably, the place used for garaging the family cars and housing the generator.

Recalling her earlier thought, she remarked, 'Do you know, I've never even *seen* a generator.'

He raised a quizzical brow. 'Does that bother you?'

'Not really... But this might be the only chance I'll ever get to have a look at one.'

'There's nothing much to see,' he said dismissively. 'It's just a machine for converting mechanical into electrical energy.'

'I know *what* it is,' she told him a shade tartly. 'The point I'm making is, I've never actually *seen* one. And I'd like to,' she added firmly.

'We've work to do,' he reminded her severely.

Something about his reluctance to show her the generator stiffened her resolve. 'It won't take long. Just a quick peep.'

Looking half-amused, half-exasperated, by her persistence, he agreed, 'Very well. The place isn't locked, so come along.'

He put the secateurs into his pocket, and, propping the spade and saw against the wall of the terrace, led her across to the old coach-house and through a side door.

Inside it was high-roofed and spacious, with a stone-slabbed floor. There were two main entrances, one of which was clearly no longer used and, at the far end, half a dozen partly screened, individual parking bays.

Long windows were set in the whitewashed walls, and close by, above a workbench, several shelves held a miscellaneous collection of tools and equipment, including a large rubber-covered torch.

'There's a torch,' Anna pointed out.

Quite unabashed, he admitted, 'Yes. I noticed it this morning. Regrettably the batteries don't seem to be working.'

Why was he always so ready with an answer? she wondered crossly.

Like a showman, he gestured towards some machinery surrounded by a high guard-rail. 'Well, there it is... Your very first generator.'

Though to Anna it looked complicated, it was a good deal smaller than she'd expected.

'Satisfied?' he asked after a moment.

'Yes, thank you,' she answered politely.

With the merest hint of impatience, he suggested, 'Then suppose we get on.'

It was too chilly to want to stand around, and she was turning to accompany him out when, from the far end of the building, a flash of sun reflected from something metallic caught her attention.

Curiosity made her take a few steps back and look more closely. The 'something metallic' appeared to be the boot of a car.

Ignoring the door that he was holding open for her, she walked along to where a silver BMW was parked. Though by no means a new model, it was highly polished and looked to be well maintained.

When she made no move to join him, Gideon let the door swing shut and walked back to stand by her side.

Her grey eyes unconsciously accusing, she said, 'Last night you told me there wasn't another car. You said they'd all been sold after your father's death.'

'I said all the *family* cars had been sold. This BMW belongs to the Morrisons.'

She half shook her head, unable to believe it. 'This doesn't look like the kind of car ordinary people would own.'

'It used to be one of the family cars,' Gideon admitted. 'But when I arranged to have the others sold, I told Arthur he could keep the BMW. He's been taking care of it for the best part of fifteen years, and it's always been his pride and joy.'

'So why didn't they go on holiday in it?' She made no attempt to hide her scepticism.

Unruffled, he explained, 'It's a long drive up to Scotland, and they had to consider both the weather and the fact that they're not getting any younger. In the end they decided to go by train.'

Put like that it sounded eminently reasonable.

Feeling a little sheepish, and hoping she hadn't vexed him too much, she apologised. 'I'm sorry, but it just seemed a bit…well…odd.'

'There's nothing to be sorry about,' he assured her cheerfully as they made their way outside. 'I don't blame you in the slightest for wanting some kind of explanation. In your place I'd have wanted one.'

Relief that he wasn't angry made her spirits rise with a bound.

Closing the door behind them, he said with a grin, 'Come on then, Mighty Mouse, to work!'

Flexing her muscles, she asked, 'What would you like me to do?'

Taking the secateurs from his pocket, he suggested, 'Perhaps you can cut some holly while I get on with the rest?'

'Certainly.'

'You'd be best keeping to this level area if possible,' he warned. 'The ground on either side of the lawn is uneven and slopes away, so there's bound to be some deep drifts.'

'Nothing I can't cope with,' she assured him jauntily. 'Unlike California, we get snow here most winters.'

He gave her a glinting look, which she answered with an innocent smile.

A young holly tree was growing on the edge of some shrubbery bordering what was clearly the lawn, a few dark-green glossy leaves and red berries visible through its shroud of snow.

Having difficulty picking up her feet, Anna advanced determinedly on the tree, and, seizing hold of a likely branch, struggled to cut it.

Without warning a veritable avalanche of snow descended on her and, dropping the secateurs, she staggered sideways.

Immediately she was floundering in a deep drift, and a moment later losing her balance completely. She found herself spread-eagled on her back with what seemed like half a ton of snow on top of her.

Blinded, deafened, and half-suffocated, she brushed the cold wet mass from her face and was trying to struggle free when she saw Gideon standing looking down at her, his expression unnaturally deadpan.

Then a corner of his mouth twitched.

'Don't you dare!' she warned him.

Giving up all pretence, his green eyes sparkling with amusement, he threw back his head and laughed.

His laughter was both attractive and infectious, and, seeing the funny side, she joined in. She was still laughing when his strong hands gripped her wrists and hauled her out.

As soon as she had regained her balance, he retrieved her woolly hat, which he shook free of snow and jammed it back on her head, then, his expression smug, he taunted, 'If you find you can't cope after all, do let me know.'

He'd only gone a short distance when a well-aimed snowball hit him on the back of the neck.

'So that's all the thanks I get for rescuing you!'

A spirited snowball fight ensued, while she backed away and he gradually advanced on her. He was within a few feet when a hastily constructed snowball, thrown a shade wildly, hit him full in the face.

'Why you little…!' He caught hold of her.

Cheekily, she peeked up at him.

Bending his head, he kissed her. At first his lips were cold, but when he deepened the kiss his mouth was warm.

Her wet, bedraggled state and her clumsy clothing were forgotten. The snowy garden ceased to exist. There was nothing in the world but his mouth on hers and a wild excitement that surged through her body like a tidal wave.

He released her slowly, his mouth lingering as though reluctant to leave hers. Then, lifting his head, he said, 'Just let that be a lesson to you.'

Unable to answer back, she turned like someone in a trance to pick up the secateurs and resume her task.

Though his words had been light, teasing, his quickened breathing and the husky note in his voice convinced her that he'd been far from unmoved by the kiss.

A kiss that, with so much thick clothing between them

and only their mouths touching, *should* have been relatively innocuous, yet had been anything but.

By the time a huge bunch of prickly holly had been gathered, the spruce boughs had been cut, and a tall, slender Christmas tree dug up, it had turned appreciably colder. The sun had disappeared, and the blue of the sky had turned to an icy pearl delicately tinged with pink.

Dusk was hovering in the wings.

'It looks as if there might be a sharp frost tonight,' Gideon remarked, 'and if it freezes on top of this lot it's bound to add to the chaos. Even if it doesn't freeze, I doubt if anything will be moving in the next twenty-four hours. It's a good thing neither of us have to go anywhere,' he added cheerfully.

Anna's common sense metaphorically wrung its hands, while, alarmingly, her reckless streak rejoiced.

Trying to banish that streak of what she recognised as insanity, and clinging to her sense of caution, she began firmly, 'If I have no choice but to stay—'

Almost managing to sound regretful, he broke in, 'I think you'll find you haven't.'

'Then there's one thing I want to get quite clear...'

He raised an enquiring brow. 'And what's that?'

'I have absolutely *no* intention of sharing either your room or your bed.'

'Very well. I'll move out.'

Anna was surprised; she'd expected him to argue, or at least try to cajole her, and his easy acceptance threw her.

'That isn't necessary,' she said hastily. 'I'll be quite content to have a blanket in front of the kitchen fire.'

He shook his head. 'You're a guest here. If anyone is going to sleep in front of the fire it had better be me. I'm used to roughing it.'

Feeling guilty, she protested, 'I don't want you to spend an uncomfortable night because of me.'

'I won't. In fact, I'll bring a pillow and some proper bedding downstairs, if it will make you happy. Now, if you can manage the holly without getting prickled to death…?'

When everything had been carried into the garden-room, seeing that she was staring to shiver, Gideon said, 'I suggest you go and thaw out now. I'll deal with the rest.'

Only too thankful to obey, she discarded her outdoor things and hung them on the pegs, before sitting down on the bench to deal with her boots.

Clinging to the wellingtons was a residue of old soil, which the snow had turned to mud, and by the time she had managed to pull them off her hands were thoroughly dirty.

There was a bathroom just along the wide corridor, but, chilled to the bone, she found the prospect of washing in a cold room in icy-cold water wasn't an appealing one.

As though she'd faxed him the thought, Gideon glanced up from planting the tree and said, 'It'll be a lot warmer in the kitchen, and if you look on top of the Aga you should find a kettle of hot water waiting.'

Wearing one pair of the borrowed socks, she padded back to the welcoming warmth and washed her face and hands in the stainless-steel sink.

Then, feeling considerably better, she found her bag and combed her damp, tangled hair, leaving it loose around her shoulders to dry.

She had replaced the socks with slippers and was sitting comfortably in front of the fire by the time Gideon had brought everything through to the kitchen.

When the fragrant spruce boughs and the bright holly had been put in place, he positioned the tree to the left of the fireplace and remarked, 'All it needs now are some decorations.'

'Have you got any?'

'There used to be a box in the cupboard in the old nurs-

ery, if they're still there. If not, we'll just have to impro-
vise.'

Stepping on to the wide hearth, he heaved the massive
Yule log into place, making a myriad bright sparks fly up
the chimney and setting the other logs crackling fiercely.

'There! That should burn all evening.'

He dusted off his hands. They were lean and well shaped,
with long fingers and a tactile strength. Exciting hands.

Tearing her gaze away, she swallowed, and said, 'When
you're ready to wash, I've left you half the hot water.'

'Generous woman.' He fetched the huge kettle and emp-
tied its steaming contents into the sink before running in
some cold.

Then, taking off his watch and his fine polo-necked
sweater, he put them aside and, standing naked to the waist,
filled his palms with water and began to sluice his face and
neck.

She noticed that his ears were neat and set close to his
head, and his thick corn-coloured hair curled enticingly into
his nape.

All at once her fingers itched to touch it.

As though to restrain any such impulse, she clasped her
hands together in her lap, and, her breath coming a little
unevenly, watched him perform his ablutions.

He looked superbly fit, with broad shoulders and muscular arms. Well-developed biceps suggested that at some
time in his life he'd done manual work. His tanned skin
was clear and healthy without a mark or blemish anywhere...

Not even on his left arm.

It seemed incredible that he could have come down on
the cobbles hard enough to put his arm out of action without leaving so much as a bruise...

As though the disturbing thought had somehow got
through to him, he turned his head to glance at her.

'Something wrong?'

'Your elbow... There isn't a mark on it.' Her voice was puzzled.

'I told you it would be good as new by today,' he said easily. 'A sharp blow on the elbow can easily affect the use, without leaving much in the way of bruising.'

Though his answer had been pat, she still felt vaguely dissatisfied, unconvinced. Yet why should he pretend to have injured his arm if he hadn't? It didn't make sense.

But since she'd met him quite a few things hadn't made sense.

CHAPTER SIX

TOSSING aside the towel, he pulled on his sweater, replaced his watch and ran a comb through his thick fair hair. 'Now, I guess the next thing on the agenda is a hot drink…'

'A cup of tea would be wonderful,' she agreed.

'As it's Christmas, I thought I'd make a spot of punch.'

'What do you put in it?' she enquired, well aware she sounded wary.

'Only fresh fruit juice and spices, and a spoonful of molasses. It's quite innocuous, I assure you.'

Blushing a little, because she knew only too well what he was thinking, she explained, 'My friend Cleo does a lethal version. I remember last Christmas just one glass gave me a splitting headache.'

'Speaking of headaches, how is yours?'

'It's gone, thank you.'

'Then you should be able to indulge in a pre-dinner sherry and a glass of wine with your meal tonight without any ill effects.'

Having made a complete fool of herself once, Anna wasn't sure if she wanted to indulge in anything of the kind.

Noting her reservation, he suggested, 'But you can always make up your mind nearer the time.'

Ensconced in her chair, her toes stretched to the blaze, she listened to Gideon opening cupboards and moving about, preparing the hot, spicy drink.

Though she wasn't looking in his direction, she was intensely *conscious* of him, aware that he was working with a swift efficiency that suggested he was well used to taking care of himself.

So perhaps there had been no live-in lover? Though that was an unsafe conclusion to draw. Even if there *had* been someone, he was hardly the type to sit and let a woman wait on him...

'Here we are.'

Anna looked up to find he was offering her a steaming mug. The smell of cloves and cinnamon she'd always associated with Christmas wafted up enticingly, mixed with that of black treacle and oranges.

She took a cautious sip and then relaxed. This punch was fruity and harmless. It was only the memory of joyful childhood Christmases with her family that was painful.

When his own mug was empty, Gideon rose to his feet and said briskly, 'Now I'd better make up the bedroom fire and see if I can find those decorations.'

Through the windows Anna could see that it was almost dark, and away from the glowing hearth shadows were gathering in the corners of the room.

'Won't you need a candle?'

'When I was in the coach-house this morning I found a couple of lamps and a supply of oil, which will be even handier.'

While she watched, he took two glass-chimneyed lamps from the bottom cupboard and proceeded to fill them with oil. Then he trimmed and adjusted the wicks before lighting them and replacing the chimneys.

The task appeared to be a fiddling one, and, surprised by his competence, she said, 'It seems you have more of the nineteenth-century skills than the twenty-first.'

Gideon pretended to look aggrieved. 'Is that a reference to my lack of ability as a mechanic?'

'It was meant as a compliment. However, if the cap fits...' she added saucily.

Wiping oil from his fingers, he threatened, 'Later on I shall extract due retribution for that remark.'

Remembering that kiss in the garden, she began to shiver with a combination of alarm, excitement and anticipation.

But she mustn't let herself react in that way. It was dangerous in the extreme. She must be on her guard, must keep in mind how potent his sex appeal was. A kiss could lead to…

No, it was better not to pursue that train of thought… Just keep reminding herself that he didn't care a fig about *her*. All he wanted was a bit of fun to enliven his Christmas.

A bit of fun she had no intention of providing.

Having drawn the curtains to shut out the frosty night, he picked up one of the lamps and made for the door.

Above the black, high-necked sweater, the glow turned his face and hair into the golden mask of some ancient Aztec sun god, a powerful and ruthless deity who could only be placated by blood sacrifices.

A fanciful thought.

But, while Gideon was no god, he undoubtedly had power and a ruthless streak. She felt instinctively that as far as his enemies were concerned he would give no quarter.

Then, shaking her head ruefully at her melodramatic flights of fancy, she made a determined effort to return to practicalities. 'While you're looking for the decorations, is there anything I can be doing towards tonight's meal?'

He stopped in his tracks. 'Oh, excellent woman! Though our "traditional Christmas fare" is just a ready-stuffed turkey roast, it's about time it was in the oven, so if you could do that? And perhaps put the pudding on to steam?'

'Of course. Anything else?'

He shook his head. 'In order to cut out as much work as possible I bought everything ready-prepared, so there's not much else to do. Unless you'd like to open some wine? As it's going to be a rich meal, I thought a bottle of Châteauneuf-du-Pape.'

She had transferred the foil-wrapped turkey from the larder to the Aga, placed the pudding basin in a steamer, opened the rich red wine and gone back to her chair before he returned with a large cardboard box tucked under his arm.

'Success!' he announced triumphantly.

Placing the oil lamp on the table, he opened the box and displayed a collection of tree ornaments.

'There's even a fat fairy to put on the top.'

Recalling the slender, ethereal Christmas fairy that had graced her own childhood tree, Anna objected, 'I don't believe there's any such thing as a fat fairy.'

'Want to bet?'

He produced a plump fairy-doll with glittering wings and a wand, wearing a net tutu and a simpering expression.

'This used to be my younger sister's favourite,' he went on with his charming, lopsided grin. 'One year when I'd hidden it she hit me with a toy truck, and I bled all over the nursery floor. Which only goes to prove the truth of the observation that the female of the species is deadlier than the male.'

'Well, I don't believe a word of it,' Anna said hardily.

He came close and leaned over her. 'Oh, it's quite true. Look, I've still got the scar to prove it.'

Though she was convinced that he'd deliberately misunderstood her, she found herself forced to look while, with a neatly trimmed nail, he pointed out a small sickle-shaped scar on his cleft chin.

His face was so close she was aware of his breath on her lips, warm and fresh and sweet. As though there was no help for it, her eyes lifted to his clear-cut mouth.

Though she knew it was utter madness, she *wanted* to feel his mouth against hers, *wanted* him to kiss her.

Perhaps her expression betrayed her, because he smiled, his white teeth gleaming.

A current of excitement ran between them, drawing them together, making them seem like two people on the verge of becoming lovers. Her stomach clenched, and heat flooded through her.

A hand on either arm of the chair, effectively trapping her there, he leaned a fraction closer; suddenly panic-stricken, she cried, 'Don't!'

His dark, level brows shot up. 'As scars go it's no big deal. Nothing to get squeamish about.'

Through clenched teeth, she said, 'You know perfectly well it's not that.'

'Ah! Afraid I was going to kiss you?'

'I don't like to be kissed against my will.'

'Sure it would be against your will?'

'Quite sure.'

'I beg leave to doubt it. In fact I don't believe you're anywhere near as cool and untouchable as you're trying to make out. But if by any chance I'm wrong, try to look on this as the retribution I threatened you with.'

His lips brushed hers in a thistledown caress, and lingered tantalisingly.

Her own lips quivered, wanting desperately to part, to respond to that light, coaxing pressure.

Somehow she kept them pressed tightly together.

With his tongue-tip he traced the outline of her mouth and the little hollow beneath; then, taking her bottom lip between his teeth, he nipped it gently.

Eyes closed, she shuddered at that erotic little caress.

His mouth moving across hers, bestowing little plucking kisses, he whispered, 'Why don't you kiss me back? You know you want to.'

'I don't want—'

With a murmur of satisfaction, he took advantage of her

parted lips to deepen the kiss and begin a leisurely exploration of her mouth, discovering the silky skin of her inner lip and the pearly smoothness of her teeth.

After a moment or two his tongue found hers and stroked it seductively, demanding a response, making her heart race and her blood sing through her veins.

Every nerve in her body sprang into life, and a core of molten heat began to form in the pit of her stomach.

Besieged by the kind of desire she'd never felt in her life before, she answered his kiss, abandoning herself freely to this overwhelming passion.

Gone, like night phantoms which had never existed, were all her doubts, her repressions and her inhibitions. She knew that if he started to undress her she wouldn't raise a finger to prevent him.

And, though he must have known it too, he drew back.

Lifting heavy lids, she found he was studying her face. His expression was coolly cynical and, with a feeling of shock, she registered that his green eyes held a touch of contempt.

It seemed that he had deliberately set out to arouse her, while taking care to remain unmoved himself.

As she caught her breath, he straightened up, and instantly the look was gone, replaced by his normal, slightly ironic expression.

Had she actually seen what she thought she'd seen? Anna wondered dazedly as he moved away.

No, surely not. She must have been mistaken. It was he who had instigated the kiss and forced a response, so why should he look at her as though he despised her?

He certainly hadn't looked at her that way when he'd kissed her in the garden. But there had been a vast difference between the way he'd kissed her then and just now, she realised.

Then, it had been passionate and spontaneous, a *shared*

experience. This time it had been purposeful, *calculated*, and he'd held himself aloof, as though wanting to prove something...

His tone casual, almost teasing, suggesting that they'd had their fun, he said, 'Well, I guess we'd better jump to it now, if we're planning to get this tree decorated before we eat.'

Unwilling to give him the satisfaction of seeing just how much he'd managed to rattle her, she pulled herself together and, muttering, 'Slave-driver,' got to her feet, albeit a shade unsteadily, and began to take brightly coloured baubles from the box.

For a while they worked without speaking, hanging a variety of trinkets and ornaments on the prickly green branches and draping them with tinsel.

Finding the silence unnerving, and wanting to dispel some of the lingering tension, Anna was trying to think of something to say when Gideon remarked, 'As children we always had a tree in the nursery. We used to decorate it on Christmas Eve.'

Only too pleased to talk, she seized the chance and asked, 'How many of you were there?'

'Myself and two sisters: Marcia, almost six years older than myself, and Jacqueline, a year younger.'

Perching a bright-eyed toy robin so that it sat tilted forward, as though ready to dive-bomb an innocent-looking dove on the branch beneath, he added, 'This brings back some of the happier memories.'

'Wasn't your childhood particularly happy?'

'It was until I was ten, then Mother died.'

'Oh, I'm sorry.' Even as she spoke Anna realised how inadequate the sympathy was. Remembering her own loss, she added, 'I suppose nothing was ever the same?'

'Not for any of us. Marcia, who seemed to be the worst hit, went right off the rails. She was still only sixteen when she found she was pregnant. Father, always the hypocrite, was furious. He made her life so unpleasant that she ran off and married the baby's father. Which proved to be an even worse mistake.

'The boy, who was only about the same age as herself, turned out to be a complete ne'er-do-well. He was sent to prison for theft before their child had even started school. They had been living in a rented flat, and with not enough money to pay her way Marcia was threatened with eviction. Desperate, she came home and asked Father for help. He said she'd made her bed and must lie in it.

'I was nearly fifteen at the time. I told him that if he didn't help her, as soon as I was old enough I'd leave home and never come back. Perhaps he thought I didn't mean it, or perhaps he didn't care. Whichever, that good, kind, philanthropist threw both his daughter and his grandson out...'

'But you *did* mean it?'

'Oh, yes, I meant it. Though I didn't like abandoning my younger sister, and I'd always loved the Manor, the minute I was old enough I packed my bags and left. With Jacqueline's blessing. As soon as she was eighteen, she followed suit. But because she'd always been Father's favourite he did at least finance her until she'd finished university.'

'How did *you* manage?'

'I took evening and weekend jobs to support myself until I graduated.'

'Then I think you said you travelled?'

'Yes, I spent some years working my way round the world before settling in California.'

'And you never came back home?'

'In the past year or so I've made quite a few trips to London on business, but if by *home* you mean Hartington Manor, the answer's no, not while my father was alive. The first time I came back here was last year, for his funeral...'

Anna sighed. Obviously Sir Ian had been a difficult man, but it seemed a pity that father and son had never had a chance to make their peace with each other.

As though following her train of thought, Gideon went on, 'Things might have worked out differently, but by the time Mary Morrison realised how ill he was and tried to let Jackie and me know it was too late.'

'Then he didn't see his daughters either?'

'No,' Gideon said flatly. 'Jackie, who's married to a professor, was abroad with her husband on a lecture tour.'

'What about Marcia?'

Gideon shook his head. 'She and her husband died in a car crash some ten years ago. To give my father his due, after their death he gave his grandson a home, at least until he started university. But when he got sent down in his first year the old man threw him out.'

Anna was just about to ask Gideon what had happened to his nephew when he closed the subject by saying briskly, 'Well, that's enough gloomy family history for one day. Now, do you think we need any more tinsel?'

Her headed tilted a little to one side, Anna stepped back to survey the tree. 'No, I don't think so.'

'Then there's just our fat fairy to put on the top.' He handed her the doll. 'As I'm feeling particularly magnanimous, I'll let you have the honour.'

'I'm not sure if I can reach,' she said doubtfully.

'No problem.' Before she could object, he put his hands one each side of her slim waist and, without apparent effort, lifted her a good eighteen inches off the floor.

Her heart lurched and began to throw itself against her ribs. Hastily she reached to fasten the wire that held the fairy in place. The instant it was secure, she said breathlessly, 'You can put me down now.'

As he set her down his hands slid round a little and

upwards, so that his thumbs brushed the undersides of her breasts.

Her nipples firmed in response to that lightest of contacts, and she knew he must be able to feel the way her heart was pounding.

Even when her feet touched the floor he didn't immediately release her, but drew her back against him, so that fleetingly she was aware of the warmth of his body and his muscular strength.

Head spinning, she made a small sound, whether of pleasure or protest even *she* wasn't sure, and a split second later found herself free.

Her legs feeling like chewed string, she sank down in the nearest chair.

'Did you enjoy that?' he enquired blandly.

When she said nothing, he went on, 'Personally, I've always thought that decorating the Christmas tree is one of the fun bits.'

'Oh... Yes...'

Glancing up, she saw that his green eyes held a wicked gleam. 'And there's a lot more fun and enjoyment to come, I promise.'

Knowing now that he was deliberately teasing her, she took a deep breath, and, making an effort to pull herself together, asked as steadily as possible, 'Such as what?'

He reeled off a list. 'Dates and figs and nuts in their shells; balloons and streamers and paper hats; money in the Christmas pudding...' His face the picture of innocence, he added, 'And of course exciting games to play...'

Pretending not to have heard the latter, she objected, 'There won't be any money in a bought Christmas pudding.'

'There will in *this* one,' he corrected her.

'Sneaky!'

'And, added to all that, I have a present for you.'

'What kind of present?' she demanded warily.

'I think you'd better wait and see. If I told you now it would spoil the surprise.'

'I'm not sure I like surprises.'

'You'll like mine,' he assured her. 'Now, what about a sherry before the meal?'

Still unsure, the previous night only too fresh in her mind, she debated refusing, then thought better of it. After all it *was* Christmas Day and, wary now, she wasn't likely to make the same mistake twice.

When she offered no objection, he filled two fine tulip-shaped glasses and handed her one before taking a seat opposite.

For a while they sat in front of the blazing fire and sipped in silence. Then, glancing at his watch, he remarked, 'Speaking of dinner, I hope you've worked up enough appetite to do it justice?'

'I certainly have,' she assured him, composed now, and determined to ignore any future attempt to bait her.

'In that case I'll add the finishing touches.'

'What would you like me to do?'

'You've done your share. Now you can just sit there and look beautiful.'

She pulled a face. 'It would be a jolly sight more useful if I laid the table.'

Shaking his head, he told her, 'It's not necessary. I can do that while—'

The chirruping of a mobile phone cut through his words.

Just for a split second he looked disconcerted, before an expressionless mask slipped into place.

Her smoke-grey eyes accusing, Anna said, 'When I asked if you had a mobile, you told me you'd left it in the car.'

His broad shoulders lifted in a shrug. 'I guess it must have been in my coat after all.'

Appearing cool and unruffled now, he crossed to where his jacket was hanging and took a phone from an inside pocket.

'Hello?... Oh, that's all right. After the snow I didn't really expect you... Good... I'm glad to hear it... No, not particularly... Well, we'll have to wait and see what the weather does... No, don't worry about it... Thanks. The same to you. See you. Take care, now.'

He returned the phone to his jacket pocket, then, without any explanation, set about finishing off the meal, leaving Anna to wonder who his unknown caller might have been.

It was obviously someone who had *intended* to come to the Manor, but been put off by the snow.

His manner had been intimate and affectionate, so more than likely it had been a woman friend. Perhaps the live-in lover she had speculated about? Maybe, unable to travel with him for some reason, she had followed on later?

Yet last night Gideon had talked as if he expected to be spending his first Christmas back in England alone. And if he *was* hoping to be joined by some woman, why had he wanted *her* to stay?

It just didn't add up. Unless he was the kind of man who would try to fill any short gap in his life with any available woman...

'Penny for them.'

She looked up to find that everything was ready and Gideon was waiting to pull out her chair and serve the food.

'Have you never heard of inflation?' She made a determined attempt to sound light-hearted as she moved to join him.

The table had a suitably festive air, with a gold candle at either end and, as a centre-piece, a posy of holly and mistletoe threaded with red ribbon.

While they ate a leisurely meal and finished off with coffee, he kept her entertained with anecdotes about his travels and, when she expressed interest, his life in California.

Rather to her surprise the only woman he mentioned throughout was his housekeeper, whom he described as a cheerful and motherly Puerto Rican.

In the end, finding she was unable to help herself, Anna asked, 'No live-in lover?'

He raised an eyebrow at her, and she was annoyed to find herself blushing.

'Well, *you* asked *me* that,' she pointed out, trying hard not to sound defensive.

'So I did,' he agreed lazily, reaching to refill their coffee cups. 'Well, my answer's the same as yours. No. I've had lovers, of course, but I've always steered clear of cohabitation. I imagine it would require a great deal of tolerance, unless the two people involved really loved each other.'

She had decided he was going to leave it at that, when he went on, 'There's only one woman I would have been willing to live with. In fact, we might have been married by now, had she been free...'

Anna was struggling to cope with a stab of pain like a knife-thrust when he went on, 'But though Eva was separated from her husband for a year before I met her, she's a Catholic and doesn't believe in divorce.'

He relapsed into silence.

While she finished her coffee, Anna watched his preoccupied face and wondered if he was still thinking of the other woman.

When she put down her empty cup, he roused himself to ask politely, 'More coffee?'

'No, thank you,' she answered with equal politeness.

Then, determined to banish Eva's ghost, she gave a bright smile and credit where it was due. 'The entire meal was delicious. I've really enjoyed it.'

'We aim to please,' he responded easily, adding, 'Shall we move to the more comfortable chairs?'

She got to her feet.

Dropping a casual arm around her shoulders, he escorted her back to the fire. Just that light, almost impersonal touch made her pulses leap.

When she was seated in front of the glowing hearth, Gideon stirred the Yule log with his toe, making it blaze and crackle, and, leaning a shoulder against the stone surround of the fireplace, stared into the leaping flames.

There was a short, brooding silence; then, with the air of a man who has determined to take a certain course of action and wants to get on with it, he asked, 'Now, I hope you're ready for the surprise I promised you?'

Though he spoke equably, there was the faintest edge to his voice, the merest hint of a hidden purpose, but it was enough to send a warning tingle down her spine.

What was he up to? she wondered uneasily. Was this yet another elaborate game?

She had almost succeeded in convincing herself that it was, when some sixth sense insisted that this was no game. Whatever he was planning to spring on her, his motives were deadly serious.

He watched the mixed emotions chase one another across her face, before she answered, 'As ready as I'll ever be.'

'You don't sound terribly enthusiastic.'

'As I remarked earlier, I'm not sure I like surprises.'

'And as I told you, I believe you'll like this one.'

When she said nothing further, he enquired blandly, 'Aren't you going to ask me what it is?'

Strangely unwilling, she took her courage in both hands and, apprehension making her sound somewhat ungracious, said, 'All right. What is it?'

Looking amused by her reluctance, he crossed to the

dresser and from one of the drawers took a large, flat envelope made of thick parchment.

'This.' He handed it to her, then, taking his own seat, waited for her to open it.

With the caution of someone expecting a trap, she did so, and, having extracted a single sheet of paper, sat staring down at it speechlessly.

Addressed to 'My Lady Eleanor', and bearing the date September 1621, it was a love letter—or, rather, a declaration of love, tender and passionate and moving, written in a clear and very beautiful seventeenth-century script.

It was signed simply 'Michael S.' The capital letters in the name were elongated and sloping forwards.

Looking up at last, Anna said, her voice scarcely above a whisper, 'It's absolutely *beautiful*.'

'I thought you'd like it. As I told you previously, I've no real knowledge of manuscripts, but this seemed eminently suitable as a gift for someone with your interests.'

Taken aback, she protested, 'But you can't mean me to keep it?'

'Of course I mean you to keep it.'

'Thank you, but I couldn't possibly.'

'Why not?'

'Because if it's genuine, and I'm almost certain it is—'

'Tell me *why* you think it's genuine,' he broke in.

'I should say both the paper and the ink are in keeping with the period, and the signature, with those long, sloping letters, seems to be authentic—'

'Then you've seen the same signature before?'

'Yes, on another surviving manuscript. It's very distinctive…'

'And if it *is* authentic?'

'Then the letter was almost certainly written by Michael Solhurst, a soldier poet who was a contemporary of Donne and Shakespeare.'

When Gideon merely waited, she added bluntly, 'That makes it worth a considerable sum of money. Even if it's a copy, which I don't think it is, it would still fetch quite a bit.'

His green eyes holding a look she couldn't decipher, he said flatly, 'It isn't a copy.'

'Do you know the provenance?'

'Yes.'

'Well, if it's part of Sir Ian's collection—'

'It isn't. It comes from the family archives. It was sent to Lady Eleanor Strange.'

Anna caught her breath, and, her eyes shining, asked, 'Can you tell me what happened? Did she return his love?'

'Yes, apparently she did. But, despite her pleas, her father refused to agree to their marriage. He had a more advantageous union in mind for his eldest daughter—her own cousin Charles. Eleanor, however, was strong-willed, and despite being confined to her room, and given only bread and water, she refused to marry Charles, declaring she'd rather die an old maid. Which, eventually, was what happened.'

Anna sighed.

'I can see you'd have liked a more romantic ending,' Gideon observed.

'In a way that *is* romantic.'

'Unrequited love? Yes, I suppose it is… Well, now I've told you about Eleanor, maybe you can tell me about Michael Solhurst?'

'Apart from his metaphysical poetry, and a few surviving letters, there's comparatively little known about his life. There's even some doubt as to when he was born, but he died in 1633 and, if the historians are correct, without having married.'

'Then, for the sake of romance, we'll assume that he remained true to Eleanor.' It was said without mockery.

Putting the letter back into the envelope with care, Anna passed it to Gideon. 'Thank you. I feel privileged to have seen it.'

'Sure you wouldn't like to keep it?' he queried.

'I'd love to,' she said honestly, 'but I can't.'

'You could use it to start a new collection for when you open another shop—'

'If it was mine there's no way I'd sell it,' she broke in almost fiercely.

He looked genuinely startled. 'I thought the whole idea was to sell and make a profit?'

'Well, of course it is,' she admitted. 'But I'm afraid I'm a collector at heart. At times I've found it hard to part with something that's really special, something I would dearly have loved to keep.'

Leaning back in his chair, stretching long legs to the blaze, he asked casually, 'Such as?'

'One of the things I was forced to sell in the end was a very beautiful letter, apparently written by John Donne to one of his parishioners.'

Gideon said nothing, but, happening to glance up, she saw that his face was hard and set, and even with the firelight gleaming in them his green eyes were glacial.

Thrown by that look, she found herself stammering, 'Wh-what's the matter? Is there something wrong?'

'What could be wrong?'

'I don't know,' she answered helplessly. 'You looked so…angry.'

He made no comment, merely asking, 'What happened to the rest of your stock?'

'The whole lot was bought by an agent for a private collector,' she said flatly.

'Did you get what it was worth?'

She shook her head. 'Knowing I had little option, he

turned the screw, and finally I was forced to sell at a considerable loss.'

Lifting her chin, she added, 'But at least it enabled me to pay off the bank loan I'd taken out and settle my remaining debts.'

'So after—what was it?—a year's work and effort, you walked away with nothing?'

'Rather less than nothing,' she told him evenly. 'What small amount of capital I started with was swallowed up.'

Staring into the fire, Gideon listened to the last in silence, his face serious and withdrawn, giving no hint of what he was thinking.

As the silence stretched, and wanting to lighten the gloom, Anna added with determined brightness, 'But that's all in the past. Over and done with. It's Christmas Day and you promised me some fun.'

He looked up. 'So I did.' Getting to his feet, the Michael Solhurst letter in his hand, he remarked, 'But I'd better put this away first... Unless you've changed your mind about keeping it?'

Shaking her head, she admitted with truth, 'I'd love to. But I can't.'

He put the letter carefully away in the dresser drawer, and, a smile replacing his former gravity, said, 'Right, let the fun commence.'

She returned his smile, pleased with her small success, until the glint in his eyes made her wonder a shade uneasily what her impetuous reminder had let her in for.

CHAPTER SEVEN

As THOUGH reading her thoughts, he grinned and suggested, 'Suppose we start the ball rolling with the one thing I consider essential to round off a Christmas meal?'

'What's that?' she asked, hoping he didn't say brandy.

'A jar of crystallised ginger.' Raising an eyebrow at her, he asked, 'Surprised?'

Eyes wide, she exclaimed, 'Staggered!'

'Think you can stand the excitement?'

'I'll do my best,' she assured him.

From the cupboard he produced a cream and brown porcelain jar with a dragon on it, and taking off the lid, asked, 'I hope you like crystallised ginger?'

'Adore it.'

'That's good. I knew from the age of eight that I could never love a woman who didn't like crystallised ginger.'

A teaspoon in his hand, he came to stand by her chair and, selecting a piece of the luscious golden sweetmeat coated in syrup, instructed, 'Open wide.'

When she obeyed, he popped it into her mouth. A little of the syrup dribbled off the spoon and ran down her bottom lip.

He leaned forward, and with the tip of his tongue licked it away as delicately as a cat, effectively taking her breath, destroying her composure, and creating a sudden tension.

Damn him! she thought helplessly, convinced that the whole thing had been engineered just to throw her.

If only she could make herself immune to his sexual attraction, but it seemed impossible to combat the barrage of reactions he could release by such blatant teasing.

His expression ironic, he watched her struggle to regain her outward poise while she chewed and swallowed the sweet and spicy delicacy.

Then, having helped himself to a piece and put the jar on the table, he asked, 'Ready for the next bit of excitement?'

Without waiting for an answer, he brought an oblong Cellophane package from the dresser, and, taking a seat opposite, passed it to her.

Pictured on the lid was a pair of Victorian sweethearts, surrounded by love knots and demurely holding hands. Inside were two clearly expensive green and gold gift crackers labelled 'His' and 'Hers'.

'Yours first,' Gideon said.

Like grown-up children, they took an end each and pulled. It snapped with a satisfying crack, spilling into her lap an 'Inspirational Motto', a party hat in the form of a narrow red and gold crown, and a jeweller's box.

Unrolling the motto, she read aloud, '"Don't be afraid to reach out and take whatever life offers you; there may be no second chance."'

Gideon nodded as though satisfied. 'Singularly appropriate, wouldn't you say?'

Steadfastly ignoring that, she tried on the crown. It proved to be much too large, and settled round her forehead like a gleaming headband.

She was about to take it off again when Gideon said, 'It looks great. Wear it like that.'

'I can just imagine what I look like,' she commented drily.

He lifted an interrogative brow. 'What?'

'A hippy? Flower power and all that?'

'With those cheekbones, it makes you look more like the bride of Hiawatha.'

Something about the way he was gazing at her made her

hurriedly transfer her attention to the box. Having peeped inside, she handed it to him, wishing him with determined brightness, 'Happy Christmas.'

He opened it, and as though they were husband and wife, said, 'Cufflinks... Thank you, darling.' Leaning forward, he kissed her lightly on the lips, raising the sexual tension another notch. 'Tomorrow I must wear a shirt and show them off.'

Thrown by his unexpected endearment and his kiss, she sat like a statue until, picking up the second cracker, he asked, 'Ready?'

Once again they took an end each and pulled.

The contents of his were similar—a motto, a crown, and a small box.

With an air of gratification, he read his motto. "'Go all out for what you want, and you'll be certain to get it.'''

When she made no comment, he smiled a little and remarked, 'Equally appropriate, I hope.'

As far as she was concerned it was a jolly sight *too* appropriate, Anna thought vexedly. Wondering if he'd just made it up, but afraid to challenge him, she stared resolutely into the glowing fire.

'Now for my crown...'

He settled the gold crown firmly on his head. It was considerably wider than hers, and sat neatly on his thick corn-coloured hair. 'What do you think?'

Head on one side, she studied the effect before answering flippantly, 'It makes you look as though you belong in the medieval swordcraft and sorcery legends, like the ruler of Camelot.'

'Well, if I'm to be King Arthur you'll have to change your headband back to a crown and your role to that of Guinevere, Lady of Leonesse.'

When, reluctant to comment, she stayed silent, he pursued, 'I'm not too familiar with the stories, but as well as

being Lancelot's mistress didn't Guinevere marry King
Arthur and become queen?'

He watched until the colour mounted in her cheeks, before turning his attention to the box.

Having lifted the lid, he said, 'Well, well, well… And it
looks almost good enough to be the genuine article.'

Taking her left hand, he slipped the sparkling solitaire
on to the third finger and smiled into her eyes. 'Now we
can consider ourselves engaged.'

Her mouth went dry.

'Bearing in mind your stated need for some commitment,
that's what I call opportune…'

Weakly, she began, 'I don't know what you mean—'

'Isn't putting a ring on your finger a necessary prelimi-
nary if we're to become lovers?'

'But we're not!'

'Of course we are,' he corrected indulgently. 'We can't
start altering the Arthurian legends.'

So this was just a game he was playing in order to dis-
compose her and amuse himself…

Her fingers still clasped in his, he studied the effect for
a moment before observing, 'Your hand's slim but strong.
A solitaire suits it.'

Then, with no change of tone, 'Was your real engagement ring a solitaire?'

'I've never *had* an engagement ring before, either real
or pretend.'

Just for an instant his face tightened with what seemed
to be anger; then he shrugged slightly and, his expression
changing to one of mockery, said, 'Right, now it's your
turn.'

Hoping she didn't sound as flustered as she felt, Anna
asked, 'My turn to do what?'

'I thought, as I'd set the precedent, you might want to
give me a kiss for it?'

With the sexual tension running so high, it was the last thing she wanted to do, but, reluctant to make a big deal out of it by refusing, she leaned forward and touched her lips to his cheek.

His voice sardonic, he remarked, 'How very cool and chaste. Is that the best you can do?'

'You wanted me to kiss you, and I did.'

'I can't help but feel you could show a little more enthusiasm if you tried.'

Rattled now, she informed him, 'Well, I've no intention of trying.'

'Do I take it you're afraid of things getting out of hand?'

She was, but, unwilling to admit it, she said, 'Not at all…' Trying to sound calm and undisturbed, she added, 'I'm feeling rather tired. In fact, if you don't mind, I think I'll go up to bed.'

Taking off her crown, as if to confirm that the game was over, she got to her feet.

Watching her narrowly, he ran long, lean fingers over his jaw. 'Running away?'

'Certainly not,' she lied. 'It's just that it's getting quite late.'

He glanced at his watch. 'Dear me, so it is! Almost a quarter to eleven.'

Ignoring the sarcasm, she asked, 'May I take one of the lamps?'

'Of course.'

'Then I'll say goodnight.'

Without answering, he rose to his feet and stretched lazily; then, having removed his own crown, went to pick up the second lamp.

'What are you doing?' she asked sharply.

'I thought I'd see you upstairs.'

'No!' Swallowing, she added less vehemently, 'Please don't trouble.'

'It's no trouble. I was going up anyway.'

Trying to keep the panic out of her voice, she reminded him, 'But earlier you said you were sleeping in front of the fire.'

'That's right, I did,' he agreed.

'So there's really no need for you to come up.'

'I'm afraid there is. For one thing, if I'm sleeping down here I need to fetch some bedding… I'd also like to clean my teeth and take a shower.'

Anna was shuddering at the thought of an icy-cold shower when he added, 'By the way, I have some good news for you with regards to a shower.'

'You mean *I* don't have to take one?'

Laughing, he told her, 'When you've heard my news you'll want to.'

'Do I take it that the generator's got a new lease of life?' she asked hopefully.

'It's not that good.'

'Don't keep me in suspense.'

'Perhaps it was the shock of this morning's cold shower that set my brain working, because later I recalled that the bathroom adjoining the nursery used to have a gas water heater.

'When I went to find the decorations, I took a look. Sure enough there it was, and apparently still serviceable, so I lit it. When I was certain it was going to be okay, I moved everything I thought we might need into there, along with a good supply of towels. It's only an old-fashioned stand-in-the-bath type shower, but at least the water should be nice and hot.'

'It sounds *wonderful*,' she exclaimed.

Smiling at her fervour, he offered, 'And, so long as you don't take more than ten minutes, I'll let you have first turn.'

'Lead me to it.'

'It's only just along the corridor from your room, so you won't have far to trek.'

Taking a lamp each, they made their way across the hall and up the stairs.

Away from the warmth of the kitchen the air struck cold, and by the time they reached a door at the end of the corridor Anna was starting to shiver.

'This is it,' Gideon announced cheerfully. 'I'll leave you to it... Unless, to save the hot water and provide a little more excitement, you'd like to share a shower?'

'No, I wouldn't,' she said, with more force than politeness, and heard him laugh as he moved away.

Opening the door into an old-fashioned white-tiled bathroom, she found that he'd been as good as his word. There was a large pile of fluffy towels, and her toilet bag and night things had been placed on a long, cork-covered stool, next to his.

It was all so *intimate* that they could have been man and wife. The thought made the breath catch in her throat and her heart pick up speed.

The heater, as well as providing plenty of hot water, had warmed the air to a reasonable temperature, and if it hadn't been for the possibility of Gideon returning to find her still undressed Anna would have taken longer.

As it was, she cleaned her teeth and showered without delay, then, having donned her nightdress and dressing-gown, gathered up her belongings and the lamp, and returned to her room.

She was pleased to find that the fire, which had been recently replenished, was burning brightly, and the air was comfortably warm.

As she put the lamp on the mantelpiece, she discovered that a mug of hot chocolate, covered by a saucer, was waiting on the hearth. Sitting by the fire, she took a sip and found it was just how she liked it.

When the mug was empty, hating to go to bed with the taste of chocolate in her mouth, she went into the bathroom to clean her teeth once more.

When she returned to the bedroom, she was startled to find Gideon standing by the hearth, his back to the fire.

'Why didn't you knock?' she demanded.

'I did, but with the tap running you obviously didn't hear me.'

He was wearing a short burgundy silk dressing-gown, and, judging by his bare legs, not a lot else. With his thick fair hair still damp from the shower, and his green eyes brilliant, he looked dangerously attractive.

Thoroughly rattled, she croaked, 'What are you doing here? What do you want?'

His eyes on her mouth, he said, 'I have a fancy to kiss you goodnight.'

Remembering only too well how he'd kissed her earlier that evening, and her own helpless response, she cried, 'No, you mustn't!'

'Oh, but I really think I must. You see, knowing what stubble can do to a delicate skin like yours, I've shaved especially.'

He lifted her hand and held it to his jaw. 'Feel,' he murmured seductively. 'Smooth as silk.'

Her fingers longed to take up that invitation, to stroke over his chin and trace that beguiling cleft.

Somehow she resisted the temptation and, snatching her hand away as though it had been burnt, said raggedly, 'I wish you'd go.'

'You don't mean that.' Taking her shoulders in a light grip, he bent his head to rub his cheek against hers.

The fresh, cedar-lime scent of his aftershave in her nostrils, she begged, '*Please*, Gideon, don't...'

But even as she pleaded she recognised that it was hopeless. Panic-stricken, she pulled away, crying, 'Why don't you leave me alone? What do you *want*?'

Smiling wryly, he said, 'Do you really need me to answer that?'

Watching the hot colour pour into her face, he went on, 'I've wanted you since the first moment I saw you, my fascinating, smoky-eyed witch...'

Sliding his hands into the wide sleeves of her towelling dressing-gown, he cupped her elbows and drew her to him.

Like some hypnotised rabbit, she found herself staring into that hard-boned face, unable to look away. The glow from the lamp burnished his hair and threw his features into high relief—the thick sweep of dark lashes, the strong nose, the sensuous curve of his lips.

'And, though you've been fighting it, I know you want me too. The attraction between us was instant and mutual, the chemistry so powerful it was inevitable that we should become lovers.'

She struggled to protest, to tell him he was wrong, but she couldn't speak, could no longer deny what she knew to be true.

But she couldn't *let* it be true!

Dredged from the depths, a weakened, but still surviving sense of self-preservation enabled her to shake her head. 'No.'

'Well, we'll share a goodnight kiss or two—you can't deny you want to kiss me—and then see who's right, shall we?'

'No, please, I don't—'

Overriding the half-formed protest, he promised, 'I won't do anything you don't want me to do.'

He bent nearer, until his face went out of focus and she was forced to close her eyes, then he started to kiss her.

His kisses were gentle, caring, sweeter than wine; kisses

that were undemanding, meant to give pleasure rather than ask for a response.

He grazed over her cheeks and her eyelids and her lips, before finding the silky skin beneath her jaw and tracing the curve of her throat to the warm hollow at the base. Only after moving up to leisurely explore the neat whorls of one ear, and the vulnerable point where shoulder and neck met, did his mouth return to hers.

She began to shiver as he bestowed a series of tantalising little caresses that alternately stroked and plucked at her lips.

Now he was kissing the way he teased—skilfully, persuasively, beguilingly, making her long to kiss him back.

Between kisses he whispered, 'You're quite enchanting... No other woman has ever stirred my senses in the way that you do... The moment I saw you I fell under a spell. Now I'm afraid I might never be free again, just fated to become more and more enslaved...'

She hadn't expected to be seduced by words, and had no defence against them. With a consummate skill, and an ease that dismayed her, he was making himself the master of both her mind and her body.

His hands slid from her elbows to her wrists, then, leaving her sleeves, spread themselves flat-palmed against her spine to urge her closer.

Though he was some six inches taller, she had long legs, and they fitted together snugly, hip to hip, thigh to thigh.

As, his mouth brushing hers, he pressed her soft, feminine curves to his hard, masculine body, her lips parted on a gasp, allowing him to deepen the kiss.

'Mmm...' He murmured his satisfaction, and while his fingers stroked the warm skin of her nape and tangled themselves in the dark silk of her hair, he began to explore her mouth with unhurried enjoyment.

She found it mind-blowing.

No one else had ever kissed her in this way. David had always been an impatient lover, regarding any but the most cursory of kisses as a waste of time. Too selfish, too concerned with his own needs, she realised now, to want to give pleasure.

Being kissed so intimately, and with such leisurely appreciation, made little shivers of ecstasy run up and down her spine and every separate nerve-ending in her body zing into life.

While her pulses leapt and her mind reeled, she tried hard to keep a grasp on sanity, to retain enough self-control to enable her to call a halt when she wanted to.

But soon she was swamped by a growing need, a desire to give in, to throw caution to the winds and abandon herself to the pleasure he was giving her.

But if she did, if she let him go on, she would be lost. The small voice of common-sense made itself heard.

Gathering every ounce of strength, both mental and physical, she put her hands against his chest and tried to push him away.

She might as well have tried to move a mountain.

'Please let me go,' she begged.

His arms merely tightened, trapping her there.

'Why? After all, you're enjoying it, aren't you?'

Too much.

'You said you wouldn't do anything I didn't want you to do,' she reminded him jerkily. 'And I don't want you to go on.'

'But you *do* want me to go on—we both know that.'

'No! If you do...' Though she left the sentence in mid-air, it was as explicit as if she'd completed it.

Smiling a little, he promised, 'I'll stop when you can convince me that you *really* want me to stop.'

Shivering, she wondered how on earth she could convince him when she couldn't convince herself?

His hands cupping her face, holding it up to his and tilting it to suit his wishes, he began to kiss her again, masterful now.

Unable to free herself from his commanding hold on her senses, and the compelling excitement of his kiss, she opened her mouth to his demand.

Having won this small battle, he savoured his spoils to the full.

While she struggled to cope with the sensations his caressing tongue was creating, one hand was busy untying the belt of her robe and slipping it from her shoulders, so that for a moment its weight hung on her arms before he eased it free and let it fall to the floor.

Through the thin cotton of her nightdress his hand began to follow the curve of her breast. Her heart lurched drunkenly, and her insides tied themselves into a knot.

Raising his head, watching her rapt face, he started to brush the nipple with his thumb, making a core of liquid heat form in the pit of her stomach.

Wondering dazedly how so light a touch could cause such exquisite delight, such a flood of desire, she made a small sound, almost like a moan.

His hand stilled, and he said, 'Look at me, Anna.' When her heavy lids lifted, green eyes looking deeply into grey, he asked, 'Do you want me to stop?'

Part of her knew quite clearly that if she said yes, and *meant it*, he would.

But she didn't want him to stop.

Over the years she had repressed her natural urge to love and be loved, built a cool, defensive wall to hide behind while she waited for the right man.

For a short time she had mistakenly imagined that David might be that man, but now she knew with complete certainty that Gideon was the one she had been waiting for...

His hands moving to grip the soft flesh of her upper arms, he gave her a slight shake. '*Do* you, Anna?'

With a sigh, she shook her head.

His handsome eyes darkened to jade. 'So there'll be no mistake. I want to hear you say it out loud.'

'I don't want you to stop.'

A strange look flitted across his face, and after a second or two, his voice level, he laid it on the line. 'If I do go on, there'll be no turning back.'

'I know,' she answered thickly.

She heard his indrawn breath, before he said, 'In that case, suppose you take off your nightdress?'

It was a challenge.

Knowing she'd come too far to turn back, she accepted it.

Pulling the garment over her head, she dropped it at her feet. Then, little shivers running through her, unconsciously holding her breath, she waited in an agony of suspense for his touch.

But he seemed to be in no hurry. His eyes moved over her slowly, appreciatively, noting that she was beautifully proportioned, with small, firm breasts, a slim waist, nicely rounded hips and long slender legs.

'You're the loveliest thing I ever set eyes on,' he said softly. 'Every man's dream come true... Your skin is flawless, and your breasts are even lovelier than I'd imagined...'

As though assessing her reaction, with a single fingertip he followed the curve of creamy flesh, almost touching the nipple, but not quite.

While she stood still as a statue in the golden glow of the lamp his finger made the return journey, pausing to circle the dusky pink areola.

Smiling at the evidence of her arousal, he went on, 'I want to kiss them, to nuzzle my face against them, to take a nipple in my mouth and feel it grow even firmer as I suckle…'

Watching the embarrassed colour flood into her cheeks, he asked, 'Does my saying such things aloud shock you?'

She nodded, and dipped her head. His words had both shocked and excited her.

'Why?'

'I suppose I'm a bit of a prude,' she admitted, adding jerkily, 'I'm afraid I can't help it.'

For a moment he looked genuinely surprised, then he began to kiss her burning face, a shower of little tender kisses.

'My dear Anna, if you really are a prude I don't *want* you to help it. There's so little true modesty left these days that I find it quite delightful at the start of a relationship.' With a crooked smile, he added, 'Though you may not be quite so modest by the end.'

She hardly recognised her own voice asking, 'And when will that be?'

'Maybe never.'

Looking away, she knew it was more than she'd expected and less than she'd hoped for.

But how could she hope for anything? He had promised her nothing, offered no commitment. All he'd said was, 'I want you.'

With her full agreement they had made a conscious choice to become lovers for one night. Beyond that nothing had been decided.

He turned her face back to his with the pressure of a single finger against her jaw. 'Having second thoughts?'

Was she?

No. Whatever happened in the future, if she was fated to live the rest of her life alone, she was going to spend tonight in his arms.

By way of answering his question she raised herself on

tiptoe and, for the very first time of her own volition, kissed his lips.

When he stood savouring that light caress, making no attempt to deepen the kiss, she ran the tip of her tongue along his lower lip and bit him delicately.

Making a soft growling noise in his throat, he gathered her close and began to kiss her with a masterful thoroughness that seemed to melt every bone in her body.

When kissing was no longer enough, he drew away a little and, in one easy movement, untied the belt of his dressing-gown and shrugged out of it.

She caught her breath.

Oh, but he was magnificent! The epitome of masculine beauty. With wide shoulders, narrow hips, and long, straight legs, his body had both symmetry and grace.

On his chest was a light sprinkling of golden hair which veed down to a taut stomach, and in the lamplight his clear, healthy skin glowed like oiled silk.

As she gazed at him, unable to tear her eyes away, he teased huskily, 'Let me know when you've seen enough.'

Feeling herself starting to blush, she stammered, 'I—I'm sorry.'

'Don't be sorry. When you look at me like that it makes me feel like a god.'

He drew her close, naked flesh to naked flesh, and, his hands on her buttocks, moulded her to him, moving erotically.

His body was firm. He used it to entice, to encourage, to invite, while he looked into wide grey eyes filled with the acceptance of the inevitable.

Tomorrow she might have regrets, but now all she could feel was a breathless anticipation, a hunger that cried out to be appeased.

Reading her need, he bent his head and kissed her. Then, his lips still clinging closely, he lifted her high in his arms.

He carried her across to the bed, pushed aside the duvet and laid her down.

She expected him to join her, but he straightened and walked back to where the lamp was. She thought he was going to douse the light and leave only the fireglow, but instead he carried the lamp over and placed it on the bedside table.

Caught in its golden radiance, she asked faintly, 'Why have you brought it over here?'

'Did you expect everything to happen in the dark?'

'Well, I...' She had hoped the darkness might hide her blushes.

'Not a bit of it, my dear Anna. I want to look at you while I make love to you, see what I'm making you feel.'

His words sent an involuntary shiver through her.

Stretching out beside her, he bent his head and ran his warm wet tongue around one of her nipples. When it grew firm beneath his erotic administrations, he took it into his mouth and suckled sweetly, while with a thumb and forefinger he teased the other waiting peak.

She gave a shuddering gasp.

Raising his head, he asked, 'Don't you like what I'm doing to you?'

'Yes,' she admitted, adding breathlessly, 'but I'm not sure I can stand it.'

Laughing, he told her, 'You'll need to stand a great deal more than that, believe me.'

He resumed his teasing, but this time his spare hand began to circle her flat stomach before moving to stroke the smooth skin of her inner thighs, his fingers tangling in the dark silky curls.

With his hands and lips and a skill she found almost frightening, he dragged from her gasps and moans and shudders of ecstasy, taking her to the very brink time and time again, without allowing her to tumble over.

If his aim had been to make her beg, he succeeded.

Eyes closed tightly, she whispered, 'Please... Oh, please...'

He drew back, and for one dreadful moment she thought he was going to leave her. Then, like a precious gift, she felt his weight as he fitted himself into the cradle of her hips.

There was no more thinking after that, just a brief discomfort, then a mindless, engulfing whirlpool of delight that caught her up and carried her along until she was drowning in a climax of sensation.

Lying spent and exhausted, little quivers of ecstasy still running through her, she felt the weight of Gideon's head on her breast and, with a surge of love and gratitude, held it to her.

His lovemaking had been both tender and considerate, as well as powerful and passionate, and she had found him deeply satisfying as a lover.

Transformed by this unique and intimate experience that two people shared, she was fiercely glad that she'd chosen not to play around, that she'd kept herself for this one man.

He was everything she'd ever wanted, the man she loved, and, though he might not love her, she rejoiced that he thought her beautiful, and that his pleasure in her had been as great as her pleasure in him.

CHAPTER EIGHT

FOR a few moments, while his heart-rate and breathing gradually returned to normal, he remained motionless. Then with a suddenness that took her by surprise, he lifted himself away and lay on his back, staring up at the ceiling.

She glanced sideways at him and in the lamplight saw that his expression was stony, his whole body tense. He looked the very antithesis of a happy, satisfied lover.

Her euphoria abruptly fading, she wondered if she'd disappointed him in some way. Taking her courage in both hands, she asked, 'Gideon, what's the matter? What's wrong?'

'It was your first time, wasn't it?' His question sounded for all the world like an accusation.

'Yes, but I didn't think...' She swallowed hard and tried again, 'I didn't think it mattered.'

'Of course it matters,' he told her curtly. 'If I'd known you were a virgin—' He broke off.

'You wouldn't have made love to me?'

'Probably not. But by the time I became aware of the fact there was no turning back.'

Suddenly close to tears, she muttered, 'I'm sorry if you're disappointed... I should have realised you'd prefer an experienced woman.'

Hearing the desolation in her voice, he said in a more kindly tone, 'I'm not disappointed. And it has nothing to do with preferring an experienced woman.'

'Then what *has* it to do with?'

'It doesn't really matter,' he said dismissively. 'I suggest you forget the whole thing.'

'I can't when I don't understand what's wrong. I need to know what I've done, or failed to do.'

'You haven't *done* anything, apart from omitting to tell me that you were a virgin.'

'I don't understand why my being a virgin has made you so angry…'

'It was the last thing I'd expected.'

'I fail to see why,' she muttered.

After a brief pause, he said, 'My dear Anna, there can't be many beautiful and passionate women who are still virgins at the age of twenty-four.'

Her cheeks growing hot, she objected, 'You make it sound as though it's something to be ashamed of.'

'Well, I didn't mean to. In fact, quite the opposite. When I was young and idealistic, I thought that when I chose a wife I would like to be the first, and hopefully the *only* man in her life. Though as I got older,' he went on drily, 'I began to doubt the feasibility of finding such a woman in this day and age. So you see, I was more than a little—' He hesitated, as though trying to decide on a suitable word, before going on, '—*Startled* to find I'd seduced a virgin.'

'Well, I wasn't trying to hide it,' she said defensively. 'I would have told you the truth if you'd asked me. Though, to be honest, I thought it was only too obvious. And I had made it clear that I didn't like the idea of casual sex…'

'I know you'd *said* so.'

She glanced at his face, and what she saw written there left her in absolutely no doubt. 'But you didn't believe me!'

'No,' he admitted. 'I thought that though you appeared to be modest, and you blushed very prettily, you were simply playing the role of an innocent… I gave you full marks for acting ability,' he added sardonically.

'You were blaming me for not telling you I was a virgin,' she pointed out with some bitterness, 'but if I *had* told you, you probably wouldn't have believed me about that, either.'

'You have a point there.' He reached to extinguish the lamp, leaving only the flickering fireglow and the gathering shadows.

Thoughts chaotic, she pursued, 'But I don't understand *why* you should think I was acting. If I was...sexually liberated, why should I want to hide it?'

'Why indeed? Now you must be tired—' his voice held a gentler note '—so I suggest you stop thinking about it and get some rest.'

It was sound advice, but though Anna was exhausted her thoughts refused to switch off, and she found it impossible to sleep.

After giving her more pleasure than she could have possibly imagined, Gideon's subsequent disclosures had left her feeling wretched and forlorn and hopelessly confused.

Why had he presumed she'd been play-acting? And why had he said that her being a virgin was the last thing he'd expected, as though he'd had good reason to think otherwise?

There were so many unanswered questions, so many unsolved puzzles...

Several times he'd spoken as though he presumed she was familiar with Hartington Manor. He'd also seemed to think that she knew a lot more about his father than she actually did...

Left with a growing conviction that he *suspected* her of something, Anna wondered what it might be.

But her brain was growing confused and weary, unable to think clearly... She sighed.

Hearing that sigh, he reached out and pulled her to him; then, his body half supporting hers, settled her head on his shoulder.

Though it was comfort of a sort, it didn't ease the ache in her heart or mitigate her sense of rejection, and for a while she held herself stiffly in the circle of his arms. Until gradually, lulled by the warmth of his body and the steady beat of his heart beneath her cheek, she began to relax.

'That's better,' he murmured and, drawing her even closer, began to stroke her hair.

His touch was curiously tender, balm to her wounded soul, and after a while some of the hurt began to ease. But when she finally drifted off to sleep she was still wondering what it was he suspected her of.

She awoke knowing the answer. Somehow, while she slept, her subconscious had gathered together the various pieces and fitted them together to make a logical pattern.

Opening her eyes, Anna saw that the pearly light of morning was filtering into the room, and a weak and watery sun was trying to struggle through a thin blanket of grey cloud.

During the night a warm front had moved through and a thaw had set in. She could hear the drip, drip of melting snow falling from the eaves, and on the window sills what had been opaque white drifts were starting to turn translucent.

In the grate the fire was burning brightly, suggesting that at some time it had been replenished.

Though no longer lying in Gideon's arms, she was close enough to feel the warmth of his body, and the length of one hair-roughened leg against the smoothness of her own.

She turned her head and was startled to find that he was wide awake and watching her, his brilliant green gaze narrowed and intent.

With his corn-coloured hair rumpled, a golden stubble adorning his jaw, and those amazing dark brows and lashes, he looked attractive enough to take her breath away and set her pulses racing.

'Good morning.' His voice was neutral, neither friendly nor unfriendly, the greeting hardly that of a lover.

But then he had never *meant* to be a lover, she reminded herself bleakly, except in the most basic sense of the word.

Thinking what he did of her, he had simply used her, and when he'd discovered he was mistaken he'd been angry, blaming her as much as himself.

She moved away abruptly, and, sitting back against the pillows, her dark, silky hair tumbled around her shoulders, pulled the duvet up to cover her nakedness.

He sat up too and, as though reading her thoughts, said carefully, 'I'm sorry about last night.'

'Which particular bit?' she asked coldly. 'Seducing me? Suspecting me of deceit? Or apportioning the blame when it was too late?'

'All three.' He sighed. 'I shouldn't have blamed you, when by rights the blame was mine alone; nor should I have seduced you, and I ought to have had the sense to realise that, sexually at least, you were as innocent as you appeared. But I had good reason to believe—'

'That I was one of your father's girlfriends,' she finished for him.

For a moment he looked taken aback; then, his eyes hooded, he asked, 'How did you work that one out?'

'You said that my being a virgin was the last thing you'd expected, as though you had *cause* to think that... And earlier you'd mentioned that Sir Ian had had a series of relationships, all with girls young enough to be his daughter, and I fit into that category...'

Gideon raised a dark brow. 'Is that all? It hardly appears conclusive.'

'More than once you've spoken as if you thought I knew him personally, and several times you've asked me how much I've seen of Hartington Manor, as though you believed I've been here before—'

'And you haven't?'

'Of course I haven't. The first time I ever set foot in the place was when I followed you in on Christmas Eve.'

The look on his face suggested that he didn't believe her.

'But after last night you *must* know I've never been one of your father's girlfriends,' she cried.

'My dear Anna,' he said coolly, 'I never thought you had.'

As she gaped at him, he added, 'I'm afraid your deductions, clever as they were, weren't quite accurate.'

'Then what had you in mind when you started to say, "I had good reason to believe"…?'

'What I was about to say, if you'd allowed me to finish, was, I had good reason to believe you'd lived with your boyfriend.'

'Oh,' she said blankly.

'Perhaps you recall telling me that he wanted you to move in with him?'

'Well, yes…'

'You gave me the distinct impression you intended to. But I presume you changed your mind?'

'Yes.'

'Why? Didn't you love him?'

'I thought I did.'

Sensing her reluctance to continue, Gideon prodded, 'You said he promised that you were, and would be, the only woman in his life?'

'Yes.'

'But you didn't trust him? You thought he might not keep his word?'

She shook her head. 'I did trust him.' Flushing a little, she went on, 'It's just that at the time I'd never considered any relationship other than marriage.'

'So what did you do when he proposed living together?'

'I told him I'd like a chance to think about it.'

'What was his response to that?'

'He handed me a key to his flat and said he was tired of all the shilly-shallying. He'd give me until the following afternoon to move in my belongings, or we were through…'

'Go on,' Gideon said inexorably.

She bit her lip, then continued unwillingly, 'I spent a sleepless night trying to make up my mind, before deciding that in still holding back I was being stupidly old-fashioned. I told myself that once we were together I'd make him so happy that he'd never want our relationship to end, and one day he might even change his mind about marriage.

'My own small flat was rented. The only things I had to move were clothes, a few personal possessions, and the books and manuscripts I'd managed to collect. The rent had been paid until the end of the month, so I decided to leave everything where it was for the time being, except for the things I actually needed.

'I was far too excited to wait, so as soon as I'd swallowed a cup of coffee, I packed some clothes and my toilet things, and took a taxi to his place…'

Agitated now, she began to twist her hands together. Realising she was still wearing the ring Gideon had put on her finger the previous night, she checked the nervous movement.

Then, spurring herself to finish, she took a deep breath and went on, 'I thought I'd surprise him. It was just breakfast time, and I kept imagining how pleased he'd be to see me so early. I let myself in quietly. Both the living-room and the kitchen were empty, so I guessed he would still be in bed…'

'And was he?'

'Yes. But he wasn't alone. He was making love to another woman. Or, rather, *she* was making love to him. Her back was to me and I saw her long dark hair…'

Some of the hurt and shock and repugnance Anna had felt at that moment came through.

'What did you do?'

'I picked up my things and walked out.'

'If what you say is true, you had a lucky escape.' There was a thoughtful silence then, his voice even, he queried, 'So when did all this happen?'

'About a year ago. Just before I came back to Rymington and opened the shop.'

Gideon frowned. 'Then I take it that later you and he got back together again?'

'No.'

'But you *saw* each other from time to time?'

'No, I've never set eyes on him from that day to this.'

Though he let it go, she got the distinct impression that Gideon doubted that assurance.

After a moment, he asked, 'Were you still in love with him?'

'I thought I was, for a while… But, after seeing him with that other woman, I knew he hadn't changed and never would.'

'So you kept his engagement ring?'

Puzzled by this fixation about rings, she shook her head. 'I've told you, he *never* gave me an engagement ring. He didn't believe in marriage.'

Firmly, she added, 'The only engagement ring I've ever had is the pretend one you put on my finger last night.'

Eyes narrowed in thought, Gideon sat staring into the middle distance, while Anna gazed her fill at his handsome profile—the strong chin and nose, the chiselled lips, the thick sweep of dark lashes almost resting on the hard cheekbones…

When he turned towards her, as though caught in some misdemeanour, she looked hastily away.

His voice even, he changed the subject to ask, 'So now

you know *why* I hadn't expected you to still be a virgin, do you feel any happier about things?'

'A great deal happier. I thought you suspected me of something terrible, but at least going to live with one's boyfriend isn't a crime. Though for a time it sounded as though being a virgin was.'

Seeing his mouth tighten, she added a shade helplessly, 'I still can't understand why you were so angry.'

'I wasn't angry because you were a virgin. I was angry with myself for not realising the truth until it was too late.'

He took her hand and held it, his thumb circling the palm. 'I'm sorry, Anna. I feel an utter swine.'

'There's no need to. It's not as if you *forced* me to sleep with you.'

'No, but I seduced a woman who had made her views on casual sex pretty plain... And, though you may not believe it, I do have some scruples.'

'I do believe it. You said you wouldn't have made love to me if you'd known...'

He smiled wryly. 'I said *probably*. But I'm only flesh and blood, and you're enough to tempt the Archangel Gabriel himself. I've never in my life wanted a woman as much as I wanted you.'

Looking into her beautiful, long-lashed grey eyes, he added with a sigh, 'Now it's too late to alter anything.'

She shook her head. 'I wouldn't want to alter anything.'

'But you'd like it to end there?'

'You said you wanted me. Do you still?'

'Oh, yes, I want you. But haven't you always hoped for some commitment?'

She'd hoped for the right man, as well as some commitment. But now she knew that, of the two, the right man was by far the most important.

Firmly, she said, 'It no longer matters.' Her voice serene she added, 'I've burnt my bridges—' *and it had been a glorious blaze* '—so, as you remarked earlier, there's no going back.'

'But would you be happy to go on with nothing more than a ring from a Christmas cracker?'

For as long as you want me… But she couldn't tell him that, so, by way of an answer, she snuggled up to him and lifted her face for his kiss.

Instead of kissing her, he ran long, lean fingers over the stubble on his jaw, making it rasp. 'Much as I'd like to take up the invitation, I think I'd better do something about this first.'

'Do you *have* to?'

'Have you ever been kissed in the early morning by a man who's in need of a shave?'

'I'm afraid not. My education has been sadly neglected.'

'Then you don't know what it's like.'

Putting up a hand, she stroked her fingertips over the roughness, following his jawline and tracing the enticing cleft in his chin. 'I think it's sexy.'

'Well, if you want *sexy*.' Bending his head, he nuzzled his face against her breasts, very gently rubbing his bristly chin against her nipples, before taking one in his mouth.

She gave a little gasp.

He stopped immediately, and asked, 'Painful?'

'*Wonderful,*' she corrected huskily. 'Don't stop.'

He laughed. 'With that sort of encouragement, I think I can promise you a host of sensations you've never experienced before.'

'What kind of sensations?'

'The kind that make your toes curl.'

Some considerable time later, after he'd more than made good his promise and she was lying comfortably in his arms, he glanced down at her and asked, 'Getting hungry?'

A look at her watch showed it was almost eleven-thirty

but, euphoric, she had never given food a thought. Now she did, and announced, 'Starving.'

'Bacon and eggs and all the trimmings?'

'Can't wait! But I'd like to take a shower first. Wouldn't you?'

'I intend to.' Jumping out of bed, he headed for the bathroom without the gas water heater.

Just the sight of his lithe, tanned body made her throat go dry. 'I wouldn't have thought you were in need of a cold shower,' she teased huskily.

At the bathroom door, he turned to say, 'As you're hungry, and I'm cooking brunch, I thought it might be quicker.'

'Well, I certainly can't imagine you'd want to *dawdle* over a cold shower,' she agreed. 'But wouldn't it be just as quick if we shared a hot one?'

Returning to the bed, he scooped her up in his arms. 'It might not be as quick, but it's bound to be more fun.'

He proved to be right.

In fact it was so much fun that it was over an hour before they were companionably settled in front of a blazing kitchen fire, tucking into generous platefuls of bacon and eggs.

When brunch was over, Gideon got up to make a pot of coffee, and feeling she needed to do her share, Anna cleared away and stacked the dishwasher.

She was in an almost trance-like mood of elation, high on a drug called love. Having resolved to think neither of the past nor the future, she was living for the moment, encased in a rainbow bubble of pure joy and gladness.

Their coffee finished, Gideon put down his empty cup and remarked, 'The snow's much too deep and slushy to take a walk, so have you any ideas about what you'd like to do on Boxing Day afternoon?'

'I don't really mind,' she answered vaguely. Just sitting

here with him was enough to make her cup of happiness overflow. 'Whatever you want to do.'

'Well, now...!' He grinned, showing white, healthy teeth, and she thought yet again how utterly irresistible he was when he smiled. 'I would suggest taking you back to bed, but I'm—'

'Exhausted?' she suggested cheekily.

Giving her a pained look, he finished, 'Planning to save some excitement for tonight. If you can bear to wait, that is?'

He cocked an eyebrow at her, and smiled when she turned pink.

After a moment, his face becoming oddly serious, he suggested, 'If I remember rightly, I promised to show you some of my father's collection of books and manuscripts?'

'Yes, I'd like that.'

'Well, though the weather has turned considerably warmer, it won't make much difference to the temperature in the study, so I suggest we put our coats on.'

Coats on, they crossed the hall to the front of the house where, through the long windows, Anna could see that despite the thaw her car remained partially buried.

There was still a lot of snow to clear, though no doubt the main roads would be passable by now and, so long as it didn't freeze tonight, tomorrow would see a return to normality. The thought was an unwelcome one, and she pushed it away.

The study was a large, light, elegant room with an Adam fireplace and an ornate plaster ceiling. Running the entire length of one wall was a series of special closed cabinets and storage drawers, with a built-in desk holding what Gideon described as a 'steam-driven' computer.

Side by side on an expense of rich, Turkey-red carpet were two long, matching desks complete with comfortable-looking swivel chairs. On both desk-tops were state-of-the-art computers and all the latest technological equipment.

Anna was impressed, and said so.

'I'm intending to use the study as my office,' Gideon told her, 'so all this stuff is newly installed.'

Taking a bunch of keys from his father's old desk, he unlocked the nearest cabinet. 'You'll find some of the more interesting manuscripts in here. As we have no electricity I'm afraid I can't tell you exactly what's where, so I suggest you just have a browse while I make a phone call.'

He sat down at one of the desks and took the mobile from his pocket. A few moments later she heard him say, 'Hi! Where are you? Yes, I realise that... I'll have a cheque waiting for you... No, I don't need your thanks; just put it to good use... Very well... Yes, do that...'

There was a brief pause, then he spoke again, his tone warmer. 'Yes, I thought the thaw should have improved matters... You are? Well, see you soon... Let me know if there's a problem of any kind.'

From the corner of her eye, she watched him put the phone on the desk, then he opened one of the drawers and, taking out a large, flat package, withdrew the contents and started to go through them.

Wondering about that 'see you soon', Anna began to browse, but without her usual keen interest.

Though she could tell almost immediately that this part of Sir Ian's collection was both excellent and wide-ranging, for once in her life books and manuscripts were pushed into second place while she thought over what she'd just heard.

There was little doubt that whoever Gideon had been speaking to was the person who had phoned the previous day, and that same person would soon be arriving here.

But if it *was* his lady-friend, after everything they had

shared last night and again this morning, surely he would be considerate enough to warn her?

Or would he? Would he actually care enough about her feelings to think of it?

And, if he did, what good would it do to warn her? It wouldn't lessen the hurt. Though it might give her a chance to hide it...

'Seen anything you like?' Gideon's voice broke into her uneasy thoughts.

'A lot.' She made an effort to sound enthusiastic.

He reached to pull the other swivel chair alongside his own and, waving her into it, asked casually, 'Any you'd particularly like to own?'

'Plenty, but none I could afford, even if they were for sale... You said it was one of your interests, so I expect you'll want to keep the collection intact?'

'It is, and I do.'

'I know it takes time and money, but have you any plans to add to it?'

He shrugged. 'That would depend. Money's no problem but, as a hobby, I feel collecting might prove to be too time-consuming. Unless I decided to turn the whole thing into a business... Incidentally, there's something I'm curious about. You mentioned coming back to Rymington to open your shop... May I ask how you managed to raise enough capital to buy all the stock you must have needed?'

On the surface his question was merely a casual enquiry. But beneath that urbane politeness she could sense an undercurrent of something a great deal more pointed and deadly.

Shaken, she drew a deep breath to steady herself, before answering levelly, 'I think I told you I took out a bank loan? The rest was what was realised by the sale of Drum Cottage—you know, the one I pointed out to you on the way here.'

'You said you loved the cottage. I'm surprised you wanted to part with it.'

'I didn't want to part with it, but when my parents were killed I had little option. I was still at university and I needed the money. At first I tried letting it, but after the tenants virtually wrecked the place and went off still owing rent I was advised to sell.'

'Even with a bank loan, and the amount raised by the sale, it must have been a struggle to buy enough things as valuable as the John Donne letter you mentioned.'

'It was.'

'How did you manage it?'

'I always tried to find out in advance what was coming up for sale, then, whenever possible, buy privately. If things go to auction it can often push the price up.'

'So how did you acquire that particular manuscript?' Gideon's voice was even, with no suggestion now of anything deeper than a passing interest. 'Tell me about it.'

'There's nothing to tell, really…'

Refusing to be put off, he persisted, 'Did you buy it at auction?'

'No. I had a contact who told me about it.'

'When you mentioned it last evening, you said *apparently* written by John Donne, which suggests you weren't sure it was genuine.'

'I was quite sure it was genuine, but because of the circumstances I was unable to prove it.'

'Why not?'

'Well, it…it came to me in a roundabout way and—'

'You mean dishonestly?'

She flushed hotly, and, stiff with resentment, said, 'No, I don't mean dishonestly! It was a private sale, and I paid the asking price for it.'

'Then I fail to see the problem.'

'The seller promised to provide a provenance, but didn't,

so, because I couldn't prove its origin, in the end I was forced to part with it at a loss.'

'Speaking of John Donne...' Gideon picked up an envelope and, having removed a single sheet of paper, handed it to her. 'See what you think of that.'

Holding it carefully, she began to read in silence. Written by Donne to one of his parishioners who was about to get married, it was a very beautiful letter on the subject of human love and divine love.

Hardly able to believe her eyes, Anna read it through twice, then studied the signature carefully before looking up.

Watching her face, Gideon queried, 'Something wrong?'

'Is this a genuine Donne?'

'What do you think?'

'I would say it is.'

'And you would be right.'

Sounding stunned, she said, 'But it's identical to the one I had.'

When he merely looked at her, she added, 'Don't you see? If this manuscript is genuine, then the one I bought *must* have been a copy. No wonder they couldn't provide a provenance.'

'You don't think the letters are one and the same?'

She shook her head. 'I'm sure they can't possibly be.'

'Why are you so sure?'

'Well if this is part of Sir Ian's collection—'

'It *was* part of his collection,' Gideon broke in. 'Unfortunately it was stolen.'

'Stolen?' she exclaimed. 'How did it come to be stolen?'

His face like granite, he said, 'I thought you might be able to answer that.'

'Why should I be able to—?' She stopped short, and then, every trace of colour draining from her cheeks, whispered, 'You surely don't think *I* stole it!'

'Didn't you?'

'No, I didn't!' Anger and agitation brought the colour rushing back. 'Apart from the fact that I wouldn't *dream* of doing such a thing, how could I possibly have had an *opportunity*?'

'My dear Anna, we both know you had several opportunities. The time for pretence is over, so you might as well admit the whole thing.'

'I haven't the faintest idea what you're talking about. If you're still thinking I might have been one of your father's girlfriends—'

'I'm not.'

'Well, whatever it is you *are* thinking, let me tell you you're totally wrong. I've never stolen anything in my life. And what would be the point of stealing something like that, anyway? If I couldn't provide a provenance it wouldn't fetch anywhere near what it was worth.'

'I understand there are ways of getting round that particular problem. Fake provenances, for example. I've even heard it whispered that one or two of the more avid and…shall we say *unscrupulous* collectors don't insist on a provenance if it's something they particularly want and they're convinced it's the real thing. So you see, that's not a particularly good defence. In any case, you told me yourself that you didn't want to part with it, so perhaps you didn't *intend* to sell it…'

'I think you're mad,' she said shakily. 'For one thing you're presuming that the document I had and this letter are one and the same. I know they can't be.'

'Why can't they be?'

'Because the one I had only changed hands a short time ago. How long have you had this?'

'I bought it a short time ago, along with some other valuable items.'

As he spoke, he put several manuscripts on the desk and fanned them out to enable her to see them better.

Staring at them dazedly, she said, 'So *you're* the "collector" who bought my stock!'

'That's right.'

'Why?' she asked helplessly.

'Because some of the things came from my father's collection and I wanted them back.'

'You're quite wrong. I've never to my knowledge bought—and I've certainly never *stolen*—anything from your father. And that includes this letter.'

'Then tell me exactly where it came from. And while you're at it—' he selected three more manuscripts and tossed them down in front of her '—I'd like to know where you got *this…this…*and *this…*'

CHAPTER NINE

As ANNA stared down at the documents one thing immediately became clear.

Watching her turn white to the lips, Gideon said coldly, 'Yes, I rather thought it might prove impossible to explain.'

Lifting her chin, she said, 'It isn't *impossible*, but it is awkward. You see, I didn't buy these things in the usual way—'

'I'm *sure* you didn't,' he butted in coldly.

'But I did *buy* them.'

'So you keep telling me.' Watching her flush, he added with a sigh, 'Isn't it about time to admit you've been lying all along.'

'I haven't been lying,' she denied with a combination of anger and weariness.

'Then why are you so reluctant to tell me the truth?'

'Because there's someone else involved.'

'You mean your ex-boyfriend?'

Her jaw dropped. 'How did you know?'

'I know everything. Or almost everything. So you may as well give me your version.'

Taking a shaky breath, she began, 'I think I told you David worked for Drombies, a firm of auctioneers and valuers?'

When Gideon said nothing, she went on, 'Part of his job was to visit potential clients, to look at whatever they had to sell and give them a provisional estimate of what it might fetch in the saleroom. He suggested that if he came across any books or manuscripts I might be interested in, he'd find out if the owner was willing to sell privately. At first I

148

wasn't too keen on the idea. I was concerned that it wasn't exactly above board, and worried that if Drombies found out his job might be at risk. But he said there was no harm being done and, so long as the whole thing was kept quiet and only cash changed hands, there should be no problem.

'One day while he was looking through what he described as a largely worthless collection of manuscripts, he found that letter, apparently written and signed by John Donne. The lady who owned the collection had been recently widowed and was planning to move to Australia to be with her daughter and grandchildren. David put it to her that as the Donne letter was the only thing of real value, it might pay to sell it privately and save the commission, which suited her very well. She let him have the letter there and then and promised to provide a provenance when she'd looked through her late husband's papers. I paid the asking price. It was a fair price, but less than I might have had to pay if there'd been stiff saleroom competition. But the provenance wasn't forthcoming and when, after a time, I asked David to find out why, he discovered that the house was empty and the lady in question had gone abroad without leaving a forwarding address.'

His face hard and expressionless, Gideon had listened to her explanation without saying a word. Now he asked trenchantly, 'And the other three? How did you get them?'

'David found them for me. All three came from the same source. They were part of a collection sold when the owner died.'

Firmly, she added, 'And, if you look, you'll find that they each have a provenance—after my first mistake I refused to hand over any money until one was produced—and there's no mention of Sir Ian having owned them.'

Gathering up the four manuscripts and replacing them in the envelope, Gideon said cynically, 'I did say provenances could be faked.' Before she could protest, he went on, 'What about the others?'

'Others? What others?'

'There are several more missing from the collection that don't seem to be here.'

'You can't *still* think they belonged to your father?' she protested sharply.

'I don't *think*; I *know*.'

'But I've told you where they came from.'

'Though I found your story ingenious, as well as entertaining, I'm of the opinion that that's all it is—a story.'

'But you *have* to believe me! I got them through David—'

'Oh, I believe that you got them through David, but I also believe that it was without his knowledge.'

'I don't understand... You're not making sense... How could I have got them *without his knowledge*?'

'When he brought you here and showed you around—'

'But he never brought me here! How could—?'

'My dear Anna, I know both of you have been here several times over the past year.'

'But I haven't *seen* David for over a year...'

As though she hadn't spoken, Gideon went on, 'You had the run of the place. Ample opportunity to take something that, with a little resourcefulness, you knew you could sell. I have to hand it to you. You weren't too greedy. Had you taken more than one or two at a time, the thefts might have been discovered sooner. Tell me, why didn't you fake a provenance for the John Donne?'

Her face white as a sheet, she said shakily, 'I don't know where you're getting these crazy ideas. I think you must be mad. If David ever came here to value your father's collection, or anything else for that matter—and I presume that's what you mean—I knew absolutely nothing about it.

I'd never set foot in Hartington Manor until I brought you home on Friday night…'

Gideon's hard face showed a mixture of anger, disbelief, and something else she couldn't easily identify. 'I have to hand it to you. You don't give up easily, and in an odd sort of way I can almost admire your pluck.'

'I don't want your admiration,' she cried. 'I want you to believe that I'm not a thief!'

He sighed. 'I can understand your reluctance to admit it, but I want to clear the air. Get things into the open. If it makes things easier, I can see how you might have been tempted. A collection you'd have given your eye teeth for… The owner dead… No one who seemed to care what happened to it—'

'Look,' she broke in desperately, 'there's always been staff at the Manor—you told me yourself that Mrs Morrison and her husband stayed on after your father died—surely *they* would know who's been here?'

'They do know. It was Mary who first suspected what was going on and warned me. She told me about the number of times David had been here, first on his own, and then over this last year with a companion. She described the woman he'd brought with him as being tall and having long dark hair and blue-grey eyes. Apparently he'd taken this woman all round the house and shown her the secret passage, as well as my father's collection of books and manuscripts…'

So that was why Gideon had expected her to know about the secret passage…

'Mary Morrison has sharp eyes, and a lot of the books might have proved a little bulky to secrete, but it must have been comparatively easy to slip a few sheets of manuscript into a handbag?'

'I wouldn't know,' Anna said curtly. 'As I keep telling you, it's more than a year since I set eyes on David, so whoever he brought to the manor it wasn't me. And if Mrs Morrison was here now I'm sure she'd tell you the same. When she gets back from Scotland—'

'I'm hoping it won't be necessary to wait that long to find out the truth—'

The sound of an engine cut through his words. A moment later a car drew up outside and they heard the slam of a door.

It seemed the visitor he was expecting had arrived.

'Excuse me for a moment,' Gideon said.

Closing the door behind him, he went through into the hall, leaving Anna sitting in the chair feeling emotionally battered, limp as a rag doll which had been ill-used and thrown aside.

Through the chaos of her thoughts, one thing was clear. Only when Mrs Morrison returned from Scotland, and that wouldn't be until after New Year, would she stand a chance of proving her innocence. Until then he would continue to believe she was a thief and a liar.

She bit her soft inner lip until she tasted blood. Thinking what he did, how *could* he have made love to her in the way he had?

But of course he hadn't *made love* to her. On his side at least love had never entered the equation. Though he'd been a caring and generous lover, to him it had been merely sex—with a dollop of revenge thrown in for extra spice.

He was a passionate, red-blooded man; she had been there and he'd wanted her. Apart from some games thrown in to smooth the sharp edges, a few honeyed lies to sweeten the seduction, it had been as simple as that.

Which explained why he'd been so disconcerted when he'd discovered she was a virgin. Having just *used* her, he'd felt a bit ashamed.

But nowhere near as ashamed as *she* felt. Not only had

she abandoned all her principles and given herself to him gladly, but she had fallen in love with him...

She had even been foolish enough to hope that he might feel something for her. That was the worst part, the bitterest humiliation of all...

Faintly, she heard the front door open and close, then the sound of voices, one of them undoubtedly a woman's.

If only she could leave this minute and never have to see him again, she thought feverishly. It would mean walking. But crawling on her hands and knees would be preferable to having to stay here and watch him smile at some other woman while he looked at her with contempt.

She was wearing her coat, but her feet were clad in velvet slippers. Her case and the few things she'd left upstairs she was prepared to go without, but she would need her boots and handbag, which were in the kitchen.

Perhaps she could fetch them and slip away while Gideon was busy with his visitor?

Anna had jumped up when she realised that he and the unknown woman would almost certainly be either in the hall or the kitchen, so there was no way she could leave without him knowing.

Though maybe he'd be glad to be rid of her now?

Almost before the thought was complete, some sure and certain instinct told her that he wasn't yet finished with her and, visitor or no visitor, if she tried to leave, he would quietly find a way to prevent her, to keep her here.

Unless she kicked up a fuss?

Dismissing the idea, she wryly acknowledged that pride wouldn't allow her to make a scene in front of some other woman who might well be his lover.

Feeling a sense of anger and injustice, her spirits at their lowest ebb, she sank down again.

Hands clenched tightly together, she was attempting to come to terms with the unpalatable fact that for the moment she was trapped here, when she caught sight of the phone that Gideon had left on the desk.

Her determination returned with a rush. If she rang for a taxi, he would *have* to let her go.

Grabbing the phone, fumbling in her eagerness, she had started to tap in the number of At Your Service when she remembered with a jolt that they were no longer in business.

No doubt there would be other, smaller firms, but she had no idea of the numbers, and no way of finding out.

Cleo... The thought of her friend was like a light in the darkness. To her very great relief, Cleo answered almost at once.

'It's me,' Anna said, speaking as quietly as possible.

'Where on earth have you been?' Cleo asked. 'And why are you whispering? I've tried several times to call you and—'

'Listen,' Anna broke in urgently, 'I'm in a spot of trouble and I need your help.'

'What do you want me to do?' Cleo's response was immediate and unflustered.

'I want you to call me a taxi. My car's broken down and I'm at Hartington Manor on the Old Castle Road. Please tell the driver to knock loudly, and not to go away again without speaking to me *personally*. It's possible that—'

Approaching footsteps made her break off abruptly and replace the phone.

A split second later the door opened and Gideon came in, his arm around the shoulders of a tall, natural blonde. She appeared to be in her late twenties, and was undeniably beautiful, with a decided chin, a generous mouth, and eyes the colour of aquamarines.

'The main roads aren't bad at the moment,' she was reporting cheerfully, 'but getting up to the house could have been hairy if I hadn't had the Range Rover. It shows signs of being a lot worse later, though,' she added. 'The sky is clear and it's turning very cold again. I think it'll freeze when it gets dark...'

Breaking off, she gave Anna a wide, friendly smile, and said, 'Hi!'

Anna managed to return both the greeting and the smile.

Stepping back, but still watching them closely, Gideon said, 'I gather you two have already met? If only in passing, so to speak.'

The blonde shook her head. 'No, I don't think so.'

Gideon gave her a sharp look. 'You said you would have no trouble recognising her again.'

'Nor will I. This just happens to be the wrong woman. The colouring's much the same, but the features and the shape of the face are totally different. I should say there's an age difference too. The other was a girl who looked about eighteen.'

Then, with an apologetic smile at Anna, 'Please forgive us for talking about you as if you're not there. But there's been some mix-up. You see, Gideon thought you were a friend of David's.'

Anna found her voice, and admitted, 'I was once.'

'But you're not the woman he brought here.'

'No.'

'I was just arriving as David and this girl were leaving. He paused just long enough to wave to me, then he drove away. Even so, I've a good memory for faces.'

'I'm glad about that!' Anna exclaimed fervently.

The blonde laughed. 'Gideon been giving you a hard time, has he? I know he was angry about the whole thing. Men are wonderful, bless them, until they get a bee in their bonnet, then there's no living with them. The trouble is, they can never accept that they're wrong.'

Turning to Gideon, she said briskly, 'I know what you've finally appreciated, and I know it must have come as a shock to you, but instead of standing there looking as if the sky's fallen in on you, hadn't you better introduce us?'

'Of course.' He visibly pulled himself together. 'But first I owe Anna a heartfelt apology.'

Once more effortlessly in charge, master of the situation, he took Anna's hand and said with unmistakable sincerity, 'I not only *accept* that I was wrong but, believe me, I'm *pleased* to be wrong.'

Unable to bear his touch, she withdrew her hand.

His green eyes narrowing slightly, he asked, 'I hope you can forgive me?'

She could forgive him for being mistaken. What she *couldn't* forgive, was the way he'd made love to a woman he'd regarded as a thief and a liar, a woman he'd felt nothing but contempt for. A woman he'd just *used*. It destroyed her pride, her self-respect. Made her feel sick with humiliation.

'That's right, don't let him off the hook too soon,' the other woman advised with a grin. 'Get a bit of your own back. Make him squirm a little first.'

Smiling in spite of herself, Anna said, 'After such a handsome apology, I couldn't be so unkind.'

The blonde shook her head despairingly. 'At one time I used to be soft like you.'

'You've never been soft in your life,' Gideon corrected her fondly. 'I still bear the scar where you hit me with that truck…'

So this beautiful young woman was Gideon's *sister*, Anna realised dazedly, and for the first time noticed the likeness.

'In fact, I don't know how that husband of yours puts up with you.'

'Michael's an absolute pet, and he loves me,' she assured him complacently.

'Which is just as well,' Gideon opined darkly. Then, to

Anna, 'I expect you've realised that this is my kid sister, Jacqueline…Jackie, may I introduce Savanna Sands, who prefers to be known as Anna? Anna's an expert on rare books and manuscripts. She ran a bookshop until recently.'

'Ah!' Jacqueline murmured. 'Now I see how the worm got in the apple… And, speaking of worms, don't you think it's about time you dealt with the one in the kitchen?'

'High time,' Gideon agreed grimly. Holding out a hand to Anna, he said, 'Come along. There's someone I think you should say hello to.'

When she tried to ignore the proffered hand, with no intention of being flouted, his fingers closed lightly, but inexorably around hers.

'I only hope it's a jolly sight warmer in the kitchen,' Jacqueline remarked to her brother as they crossed the hall. 'It's a wonder you're not frozen. Why on earth didn't you join the annual Christmas bash at Michael's parents? Dainton Lodge is only a few miles the other side of town, and there's loads of room. It would have been better than staying here alone.'

'Ah, but I wasn't alone.'

Gideon's sidelong glance at Anna made her cheeks grow hot, and she pulled her hand free.

'I meant *both* of you.'

He smiled a little. 'It just wouldn't have been the same.'

Seeing the younger woman's discomfort, Jacqueline tactfully let the subject drop.

When Gideon opened the kitchen door, taken completely by surprise, Anna stopped short, and stood like someone in a trance while he helped her off with her coat. Her whole attention was focused on the tall, blond man standing on the hearth, his back to the fire.

'This is my nephew,' Gideon said smoothly. 'But as you two already know each other there's no need for a formal introduction.'

For a second or two she failed to understand. Then, like shaking a kaleidoscope, all the various pieces, including that elusive likeness, fell into place to make at least some kind of sense.

Judging by David's face his shock was even greater, and nothing made any sense. His mouth a little open, his expression stunned, he stared at her as though she were a ghost.

Then, his mouth closing with a snap, he snarled, 'What the hell are you doing here?'

'Keep a civil tongue in your head,' Gideon ordered curtly. 'Anna is here as my guest.'

'I don't know how... I mean, I—I wasn't aware you'd ever met each other...' David stammered.

'We hadn't until Christmas Eve.'

Sounding nonplussed, the younger man insisted, 'But as far as I was concerned she'd disappeared without a trace. How did you find out where she was?'

'Having decided when I finally came home that your ex-girlfriend had a lot of explaining to do, I took steps to trace her.'

'Well, no matter what she's told you, don't believe a word of it,' David blustered. 'She's a lying, two-timing little bitch and—'

Anna gasped.

'I told you to watch your tongue.' Gideon's command cracked like a whip.

'But you know what she's like...' The bluster had changed to a whine. 'You know how she took me for everything I'd got and then ran out on me. You know how Grandfather's manuscripts disappeared...'

'I know *your* version of events. But, surprise, surprise, your story doesn't tally with Anna's. In fact, the only thing you're both in agreement about is that *she* walked out on *you*. For instance, you said you'd met a girl you wanted to marry and, when I asked who she was, you told me all about Anna. You swore that you intended to mend your ways, and on that understanding I loaned you a large sum of money to buy her an engagement ring. After Mary Morrison told me about the missing manuscripts—including those visits you'd made with your girlfriend—and I asked to meet Anna, you claimed that she'd just upped and left you, taking the ring. Now, that was only a matter of months ago and Anna tells me that, far from mending your ways, after you'd asked her to live with you she found you in bed with another woman. She denies ever having had a ring, let alone *keeping* it, and says she had never set foot in the Manor until Christmas Eve. Furthermore, she assures me that it's more than a year since the pair of you split up.'

Looking defiant, the younger man insisted, 'Well, I've told you she's an out-and-out liar.'

'I am most definitely not!' Anna interjected, outraged.

'One of you certainly is. Though I doubt if it's Anna.' Gideon laid a comforting hand on Anna's shoulder, which she shook off immediately.

'So she's got to you, too?' David jeered. 'I always thought she was—' Seeing a white line appear around Gideon's mouth, he broke off abruptly.

After a moment, when no one spoke, he muttered, 'I suppose I shouldn't have said that. But women like her can act the innocent, twist a man around their little finger, and when there's no actual proof—'

'Ah, but there *is* some actual proof. Jackie saw the girl you brought here, and she's convinced it wasn't Anna.'

'She only saw her for a split second. She couldn't possibly be sure.'

'I'm quite sure,' Jacqueline said calmly. 'And when Mary Morrison gets back—'

'Oh, her! Apart from the fact that she's always disliked

me, she'll swear to anything to keep in the new master's good books,' David said nastily.

Then, evidently realising he'd overstepped the mark, he mumbled, 'Sorry. But I get so frustrated when no one will listen to the truth.'

Gideon dropped a hand on his shoulder. 'I'm not only prepared to *listen* to the truth, I'll do whatever it takes to *get* the truth out of you,' he declared with silky menace.

As the younger man blenched, he added, 'So I think, in order to spare the ladies' feelings, we'd better have our…little talk…in the study.'

'It's all right,' Jacqueline said with cheerful unconcern. 'I don't mind a spot of bloodshed in a good cause.'

Upset and anxious, Anna had began, 'Oh, but—' when a speaking look from the other woman silenced her.

'Suppose we get it over with?' Stepping back, Gideon gestured for the younger man to precede him.

Looking badly frightened now, David appealed to his aunt. 'You're not going to stand by and let him beat me up?'

'You're every bit as big as he is,' she pointed out calmly.

It was true that both men were much the same height and weight, but against Gideon's mature width of shoulder, his air of toughness and determination, the younger man looked soft and spineless.

As though to prove it, he almost whimpered, 'But you know as well as I do that I won't stand a chance. Don't you care about me at all?'

'As a matter of fact I do. That's why I think it's high time someone straightened you out before you get into more serious trouble. Ever since the old man disowned you, you've been taking Gideon for a ride. Instead of standing on your own two feet, you've begged and borrowed, sponged off him shamelessly. I've tried to warn him what you were like, but he wouldn't listen. He's been far too generous, too soft with you altogether...'

Gideon raised a dark brow at her.

Jackie ploughed on regardless. 'I know you've had it hard in some ways, and I'm fond of you... In fact *too* fond to stand by and see you turn into a real bad lot—'

'But I'm not—'

Taking no heed of David's attempt to protest, she continued to flay him with her tongue. 'You've lied and schemed and cheated. Now it seems you're even willing to steal. Or are you going to try and pretend this other dark-haired woman was the culprit?'

'All right,' he burst out. 'So I did take the blasted manuscripts. If that old bat hadn't kicked up such a fuss no one would even have noticed.'

Then, to Gideon, 'It was no skin off your nose. You've made a fortune in the States as well as inheriting Grandfather's estate. I'm a Strange too. I should at least have been given a proper allowance. The old devil had no right to turn me out without a penny.'

'He had every right,' Gideon disagreed icily. 'He'd paid for your schooling and sent you to a good university. You'd been given the opportunity to make something of yourself, but thanks to your wild ways you got sent down.'

'They kicked up a lot of fuss about nothing,' David grumbled.

Gideon's face hardened. 'I'd hardly call drinking and gambling and smuggling in a succession of women *nothing*. You broke all the rules of acceptable behaviour, and you've been doing it ever since.'

'Oh, don't sound so damned sanctimonious,' David cried. 'Have you never broken any rules? Done things you maybe shouldn't have done?'

'Yes. I've made plenty of mistakes in my life. Who hasn't? But I've never made a habit of lying and cheating;

I've never taken anything that wasn't mine; and, even more important, I've never involved an innocent person in my schemes. You lied to Anna, cheated her, *knowingly* put her in the position of handling stolen property... And then, to save your own skin, you tried to make out that she was a thief.'

'When you suddenly asked me about the manuscripts, I panicked... Debbie, the girl who'd been with me, wasn't unlike Anna in colouring, and you thought I was still with Anna, so—'

His green eyes glacial, Gideon said, 'So putting the blame on a woman you hadn't seen for more than a year, and never expected me to find, no doubt seemed the ideal solution...' Then, curtly, 'What happened to this Debbie?'

'She knew I'd taken the manuscripts, and the little bitch tried to blackmail me.'

'What did you do?'

'I lost my temper and slapped her...'

Looking disgusted, Gideon queried, 'And?'

'I told her that if she said a word, I'd swear it was *she* who had taken them. The next day while I was at work she packed her bags and left, taking everything of value she could lay her hands on. I told you about that.'

'But you made me believe it was Anna.'

'Oh, *David,*' Jacqueline exclaimed, 'how could you!'

'I had no option,' he muttered sullenly.

Turning to Anna, she said with a sigh, 'You really must hate our family.'

Anna shook her head. 'I'm just relieved you know the truth, and glad that Gideon's got at least four of the manuscripts back.'

'Speaking of manuscripts—' Gideon addressed his nephew '—what happened to the others?'

'I managed to sell a couple. The ones I hadn't got rid of, Debbie tore up. It's a pity I ever met the vindictive little trollop,' he added viciously. 'If I hadn't, Anna would have moved in with me and things might have been different—'

'You mean you could have continued to palm her off with stolen goods so you'd have a source of extra income to help finance your high living?'

When David, looking shamefaced now, stayed silent, Gideon pursued, 'So I take it Debbie was the woman you were in bed with when Anna came round?'

'Yes.'

'Incidentally, why didn't you tell me when Anna first walked out on you?'

'I thought you might ask about the ring.'

'And as there never *was* a ring...where did such a large amount of money go to?'

'Well, I—'

'Let me guess... To pay gambling debts, no doubt?'

'I'd had a run of bad luck and Joey was threatening to turn nasty.'

'And I suppose your latest plea for money is also due to "Joey threatening to turn nasty"?'

David's face was answer enough.

'Well, I've got news for you. I'm through paying your gambling debts, and you can go back to Joey and tell him so.'

His face a sickly grey colour, David stammered, 'No! No, I—I can't. You *promised* me a cheque.'

'That was when I believed you wanted money to start your own business.'

'I can't see that it matters *what* it's for. You've got more money than you know what to do with.'

'And apart from the relatively modest amount your grandfather left, which I've put on one side for you, I *earned* every penny of it.'

David's cockiness returned with a bound. 'Well, if

you're giving me what Grandfather left, I'll use that to pay Joey.'

'You will not. I'm putting it in trust for you until you reach the age of thirty. By that time you might have learnt a little sense.'

'But if I don't pay what I owe I may not *live* to be thirty. You don't know what Joey's boys are like. They're already getting impatient...'

Jacqueline grimaced. 'So that's why you left town in such a hurry and joined us at Dainton. I wondered what had made you suddenly opt for a family Christmas in the wilds.'

'I was trying to gain a little time,' her nephew admitted hoarsely. 'But if I'm not back by tomorrow, they'll come looking for me...' He broke off with a shudder. 'Gideon, *please*... You've just *got* to help me!'

'Very well, on certain conditions, I'll pay your gambling debts this one last time—'

'Thanks, I—'

'Don't thank me until you've heard what the conditions are. They may not be acceptable. Firstly, you will apologise to Anna.'

His face a little red, and without looking at her, David mumbled, 'I'm sorry.'

'Hardly a gracious apology,' Gideon remarked coldly. Then, to Anna, 'What do you think? Will it do, or not?'

Looking at David in disbelief, as though she couldn't possibly imagine how she'd ever loved him, she said, 'It'll have to do.'

Fixing his nephew with a steely look, Gideon went on, 'Secondly, as I hope and believe you're weak rather than wicked, I want you to get right away, leave London and Joey's casino behind you.'

'How do I do that?'

'I gather you don't like your present job, so I'm offering

you a chance to help run the American side of my computer software business. Though I can do a lot over the internet, it would be handy to have a man I can *trust* on the spot. You'll find the pay is good, and there's a house goes with the job. The Californian lifestyle should suit you, so long as you try to keep your excesses under control—'

'It sounds wonderful,' David burst out eagerly.

Ignoring the interruption, Gideon continued, 'Thirdly, a little at a time and from your wages, you will repay Anna every penny she has lost through being involved in your dishonest schemes. If you agree to these conditions, I'll book you a flight and you'll leave for the States as soon as your affairs at this end are settled.'

'I agree.'

Taking a folded cheque from his pocket, Gideon passed it to his nephew. 'Will that be enough to cover everything?'

'In the circumstances, it's more than generous,' David admitted, his relief obvious.

'Just one word of warning. Though you're family, and both Jackie and I are still fond of you, this is your last chance. Make a go of it, and the world's your oyster. Mess it up, and you're out. On your own. Understand?'

'Yes, I understand. I won't let you down.'

'Well, on that satisfactory note,' his aunt said cheerily, 'suppose we get back to Dainton and join the others? I told them we wouldn't be more than an hour or so. In any case, I'd like to get home before it freezes.'

Turning to Gideon, she suggested, 'What about you and Anna coming back with us? I know you'll be more than welcome.'

'Thanks, but I think not.'

As they turned to the door, having quickly weighed up the pros and cons, and unwilling to be left alone with Gideon in case no taxi turned up, Anna asked hastily, 'Are you by any chance going through town? If you are, could you possibly give me a lift?'

Looking more than a little surprised, Jacqueline said, 'Of course, if that's what you want.'

'I'd prefer it if you'd stay,' Gideon said evenly. 'I'd like to talk to you.'

Avoiding his eyes, Anna shook her head. 'I really must go. I've things to do.' Then, to Jacqueline, 'Can you hang on a couple of minutes while I collect my belongings?'

'Certainly.'

Having pulled on her coat and boots, Anna gathered up her bag and hastened upstairs, leaving the others to exchange a few more words as they sauntered across the hall.

While she pushed her clothes into her case, she found herself wondering why, after that token objection, Gideon had let her go so easily.

But perhaps, having thrashed everything out to his satisfaction, he had no further interest in her? Or maybe, having misjudged her and inadvertently done her more wrong than David had, he felt uncomfortable and was only too willing to see the back of her?

Whichever, she was more than pleased to be able to get away.

CHAPTER TEN

WHEN, a minute or so later, she descended the stairs, Anna saw to her surprise that the spacious panelled hall was empty.

Had they gone back to the kitchen for some reason? Or were they waiting in the car?

A quick peep in the kitchen showed it was empty, though the fire had been made up.

She was making her way back across the hall when the study door opened and Gideon emerged, the mobile phone in his hand and a slightly wary look on his handsome face.

Dropping the phone into his pocket, he came towards her and took the case out of her hand. 'Allow me.'

Unwilling to go without a word, she said stiffly, 'I'd better say goodbye, and thank you for Christmas.'

'Then while we're being so formal,' he mocked, 'perhaps I'd better say it was nice having you.'

Watching her face flame with colour, he added sardonically, 'It's pleasant to find a guest, even a reluctant one, with such good manners... Though, as it happens, making your farewells is a little premature.'

'What do you mean *premature*?'

'I'm afraid they've gone. Jackie said to tell you—'

'I don't believe it.'

Hurrying to the front door, Anna pulled it open. Dusk had already started to gather over the snowy scene. Between the black skeletal trees the sky was a clear light blue with a single shining star, and the air was bitterly cold.

The only vehicle there was her own, still partially buried.

Tyre marks in the snow showed where the Range Rover had turned and driven away.

'But she promised to wait…' Anna protested helplessly.

'I persuaded her not to. I explained that there were important things we needed to talk about, and I wanted you to stay.'

'As far as I'm concerned there's nothing left to talk about, and I don't want to stay.'

She tried to take back her case, but he refused to relinquish it and, reaching past her, closed the door with his free hand.

Turning on him like a fury, she cried, 'I've told you, I've no intention of staying.'

'And I've no intention of letting you go until you've at least listened to what I have to say.'

'I don't want to listen to *anything* you have to say. I'm leaving now, this instant.'

'Then you're prepared to walk back to town?'

'If necessary.'

He was nothing if not quick. 'So you did use my phone. I thought it wasn't exactly where I left it. Who did you call?'

'There should be a taxi here any minute. I'm setting off now to meet it,' she added defiantly, 'and you can't stop me.'

His green eyes glinted. 'I shouldn't bet on it.'

'You can't keep me here against my will!' But even as she spoke she knew that he *could*. He was quite capable of it.

Made desperate by the thought, she told him, 'If you don't let me go, when the taxi gets here I'll ask the driver to call the police.'

He raised a quizzical brow at her.

'I mean it,' she warned, clutching her bag. 'I want to leave.'

'Then before the taxi arrives I'll have to make you change your mind, make you want to stay.'

Before she realised his intention, Gideon tossed the case aside, pulled her close, and, taking her face between his palms, began to kiss her.

Her bag slipped from her shoulder and fell unheeded to the floor.

That first night when he'd kissed her at the door, it had been light, easy, a Christmas kiss beneath the mistletoe. Even so it had shaken her profoundly.

Now he kissed her as a man kissed a woman when they'd been lovers. Deeply, passionately, reaffirming his ownership.

While his mouth claimed hers, his hands slid beneath her coat and began to move over her slender body, moulding it to his, soft curves to hard muscle.

Everything in her responded to his kiss, the touch of his hands—and, disturbed to her very soul, she found her sense of purpose undermined, her resolution weakening.

But, no, she couldn't, *wouldn't* stay. After all that had happened, her pride, her self-respect, the remembrance of her humiliation wouldn't let her.

Gathering every last ounce of will-power, she tore herself free and, shaking like a leaf, stooped to pick up her bag.

'Why don't you leave me alone?' she demanded bitterly. 'Haven't you and your precious nephew done enough?'

'More than enough,' Gideon admitted soberly. 'And I'm a great deal more to blame than he is. That's one of the reasons I want you to stay. I have to find out how best to make amends.'

'I'm not asking you to make amends. I just want you to let me go. I never want to set eyes on you again.'

Just as she finished speaking, Anna heard the unmistakable sound of an engine, and the crunch of tyres on the now crisp snow. A moment later a vehicle was drawing to a halt outside.

The taxi at last. She sent a silent and fervent *thank you* to Cleo.

Giving her a quick, assessing glance, Gideon opened the door and stood, legs slightly apart, his air casual, his big frame effectively blocking the doorway.

She heard the slam of a car door, then Gideon explaining politely, 'I'm afraid you've been called out unnecessarily. However, I'll be happy to make it right with you.'

Sounding affronted, a man's voice said shortly, 'Surely you can see this isn't a taxi?'

That voice, an authoritative one, used to speaking out, used to being listened to, was oddly familiar.

Paul!

'I do beg your pardon,' Gideon apologised with smooth mockery, 'but as we were expecting a taxi it was a natural mistake. What can I do for you?'

'I've come to take Anna home.'

'How very kind of you. But I'm afraid you've had a wasted journey.'

'What do you mean, a wasted journey?'

The air crackled with male hostility.

'I mean she doesn't want to go home.'

'Look here, I insist on talking to Anna. Where the devil is she?'

'It's all right, I'm here.' Anna made a determined effort to brush past Gideon.

He moved aside, but instead of allowing her to walk away, he put an arm around her waist and kept her there.

Facing the balding, heavily built newcomer, gratitude and confusion mingling, she said a shade breathlessly, 'Thank you so much for coming, Paul. Though I really don't understand why Cleo bothered *you* on Boxing Day.'

'It seems she couldn't get a taxi, and both she and Alan

had had too much wine with their lunch to risk driving, so she called me…'

Paul was a teetotaller.

'I'm sorry to have taken so long, but Cleo said you were in some kind of trouble, so in case there was a problem I thought it best to drop Sophie off at her house on the way here.'

Eyeing Anna's coat and bag, he added briskly, 'I take it you're ready to leave? It's starting to get icy, and the drive up to this place is tricky enough as it is.'

A quick glance at Gideon's grim expression making her decide to abandon her case for the time being, she answered, 'Yes, I'm ready.'

With an air of triumph, Paul opened the door of his Mercedes for her.

But when Anna would have stepped forward, with a sudden unexpected movement Gideon folded both arms around her and drew her back against his muscular body, trapping her there.

'Please let me go,' she said coldly.

Nuzzling aside the smooth fall of dark silky hair, he kissed her nape. 'Don't be mad with me, darling.'

'Don't call me darling,' she snapped at him, trying to break free.

He held her easily, effortlessly.

'I insist that you let me go,' she said again. 'I want to leave with Paul.'

'Let her go this minute,' Paul ordered, taking a step forward. 'Otherwise—'

Gideon laughed softly, dangerously. 'Otherwise?'

A tall, imposing figure, used to commanding respect in the courtroom, Paul looked put out by the other man's refusal to be intimidated. 'Otherwise I may have to call the police.'

Sounding cheerfully unconcerned, Gideon said, 'Call the

police by all means, but I doubt if they'll be interested in a lovers' tiff. And that's all this amounts to.'

In a strangled voice, Paul began, 'Are you trying to tell me—?'

'That Anna and I are lovers? I'm not *trying* to tell, I *am* telling you.'

'I don't believe a word of it,' Paul said stoutly. 'I've know Anna for some time now, and I've never seen you before in my life. I don't even know your name.'

'It's Strange. Gideon Strange. And you are?'

'Paul Manley.' Then, returning to the attack, 'How long have you and Anna known each other?'

'Quite a short time,' Gideon admitted. 'But the attraction was instant and mutual. Wasn't it, darling?' He rubbed his cheek against Anna's.

'No, it *wasn't*,' she denied sharply.

Gideon sighed. 'I'm afraid she's still angry with me. But use your eyes, man. If you know Anna well, you'll know that's her car…'

As Paul glanced at the Vauxhall, Gideon added, 'As you can see by the amount of snow on it, it's been parked here since Christmas Eve, when she drove both of us home. Apart from a brief visit from my sister and nephew, we've been here alone the whole time. You can ask Anna if you don't believe me.'

'Is this true?'

'Well, yes, but—'

'And, while you're at it, ask her whether we've shared a bed for the past two nights.'

Anna flushed scarlet.

Paul, who was no fool, and used to drawing his own conclusions, said, 'That may be true, but it doesn't neces-
~~ily mean she wants to stay with you now.'

~~ink you'll find she does… At least, when she's got

over her pique… Otherwise why would she have accepted my ring?'

Briefly, Gideon displayed the ring, before covering Anna's hand with his own.

'But that's only—' she began.

'Believe me, this is all a storm in a teacup,' Gideon broke in firmly.

Then urgently, to Anna, 'Stay and listen to what I have to say, and I give you my word that when you've heard me out, if you still want to leave I'll take you home myself.'

'In what?' she asked tartly.

'I'll borrow Arthur's BMW. The keys are in one of the dresser drawers. *Please*, Anna…'

She hadn't expected a man like him to beg, and it threw her totally.

As she hesitated, he released her and stepped back.

Free to leave, she stood quite still, biting her lip, undecided.

Looking more than a little exasperated, Paul said, 'It'll soon be dark and it's starting to freeze, so I'd like you to make up your mind one way or the other.'

'She'll stay,' Gideon said.

'Anna?' Paul queried.

She nodded.

Mouth tight, he turned away.

He was a nice man and, grateful for his concern, she said sincerely, 'Thank you, Paul. I really do appreciate all the trouble you've gone to. Will you please thank Cleo for me and give her my love? Tell her I'll see her soon.'

'Quite sure you want to stay?'

Wondering what Cleo would think, what conclusions she would draw, Anna said, 'Quite sure.'

Paul raised a hand in salute, and she waved as he drove away, snow crunching beneath the tyres.

In truth she was anything but sure, she admitted to herself, as Gideon closed the door against the cold and accompanied her back to the warmth of the kitchen.

A seething mass of doubts and uncertainties, in some ways she would rather have said *finis* to the little episode and walked away with what remained of her pride intact.

But she had been unable to, and now she was trapped here, while Gideon dragged up things she had no wish to resurrect.

The fire was burning merrily, the crackling logs smelling of pine. Discarding her coat, she sank down in the chair that she'd come to think of as hers, and held out slim hands to the blaze.

He sat down opposite, and, his eyes on her face, said, 'I'm glad you decided to stay. I need to talk to you.'

The only thing *she* needed, Anna decided wearily, was to forget the whole episode, wipe out these last three days as though they'd never been, and with them all recollection of Gideon Strange...

No, that wasn't true. In the first wave of hurt and anger she had wanted to do that, but now she'd had a change of heart.

Before she had met him she'd never known such happiness, such joy and delight, never known what it was like to *really* be in love. They were precious gifts, even if fleeting, and well worth remembering.

She had accepted the fact that Gideon didn't love her, so surely she could accept the fact that he'd thought her unprincipled without letting it sour what had been a wonderful experience...?

As though following her train of thought, he asked, 'Shall we start with the more personal aspect?'

Her soft lips firmed. 'There's no point in raking over the ashes. It's too late to alter anything.'

'Just tell me one thing... Why, when everything had been sorted out, were you so desperate to escape?'

'By *sorted out*, I suppose you mean when you no longer believed I'd stolen your father's manuscripts?'

'So it still rankles?'

'What rankles is that you *used* me.'

'*Used* you?' He sounded staggered.

'You took me to bed out of revenge, thinking I was a thief and a liar, feeling nothing but contempt for me—'

'That's not true,' he broke in urgently. Then, with a sigh, 'Perhaps I was wrong. Suppose we leave the emotional side for the time being? Take a look at the strictly practical.'

When she said nothing, he went on, 'I expect that after the holiday you'd like to get back to work?'

'If you mean start the job you offered me, the answer's no. I don't want to work for you.'

'That's not what I meant.'

'Of course not. How stupid of me. The offer wasn't genuine. You wouldn't have asked a woman you thought you couldn't trust to work for you...'

Patiently, he said, 'If you'd just listen to me for a minute?'

'Very well.'

'Tomorrow we'll open up your shop and see that all the stock is replaced on the shelves, including the manuscripts you bought in good faith.'

'As I've already told you, all the money you paid for it has gone to settle my debts. I've nothing left to buy back the stock.'

'You don't have to *buy* it back.'

'I don't want your charity,' she said coldly.

'Charity doesn't come into it. I paid a lot less for that stock than it was worth, as well you know.'

She started to shake her head. 'It's no use—'

'Don't be stubborn. I *owe* you. Look, Anna, I'm deeply

concerned about the way I treated you, and where possible I intend to put things right.'

'Thanks, but I don't want either your concern or your good intentions.'

'All I was offering was a just solution.'

'It wouldn't work.'

'Why wouldn't it work?'

'Because the lease is up and I can't afford to pay the higher rent that Deon Enterprises are asking.'

'Suppose they weren't asking such a high rent?'

'But they *are*, and there's no chance of them lowering it.'

'I'm quite sure there is.'

Something about his certainty made her look at him sharply. A sudden suspicion taking shape, she asked, 'Do you happen to know who owns the company?'

'Yes.'

'Don't tell me. Let me guess... *You* do.'

'That's right.'

'I take it that's not a coincidence?'

'No, it isn't.'

'Surely you didn't buy the whole complex just to give you control over my rent?'

He shrugged. 'I like to hold all the cards.'

Her voice not quite steady, she asked, 'How long have you been hovering, waiting to pounce?'

'Since the detective I hired managed to trace you to Rymington.'

A shiver ran down her spine. 'What exactly were you planning to do?'

'Apart from making sure your business didn't succeed, I wanted to find some way to punish you for the way you'd treated David. I decided, in order to do that, I needed to get to know you, to see what kind of woman you were.'

'I thought you already knew,' she said with some bitterness.

'While I was stupid enough to believe most of what David told me, I like to check things out for myself. With that in mind, I timed my homecoming to coincide with the closing of your shop. I intended to make contact somehow, and offer you a job—'

'So you lay in wait for me and faked the accident! It *was* faked, wasn't it?'

'Yes. It was a last-minute idea that worked. You see, I wanted to get you to the Manor and, if possible, keep you here for a day or two. The weather was an unlooked-for bonus. It might have proved a great deal more difficult if it hadn't been for the snow. As it was, luck was on my side all the way. Though you were going to your friend's, she wasn't actually *expecting* you... The phone lines were down—'

'And my car wouldn't start.'

'Well, there I had to help luck along a bit.'

Her jaw dropped. 'You tampered with it!'

'While you were looking at the library,' he admitted unrepentantly.

'You said you didn't know much about machinery.'

'I don't. Apart from cars. While I was working my way through college, I got a part-time job in a garage.'

'All that planning and scheming just to keep me here. It was an awful lot of trouble to go to...'

'It was worth it.'

'So from the word go it was part of your plan to seduce me?'

'No, it wasn't, not at first. I hadn't meant to bring sex into it at all.'

'Then why did you kiss me at the door?'

He sighed. 'That was pure impulse. I guess I just wanted to, and I was curious to see how you'd react. Originally all

I'd hoped to do was pressure you into admitting what you'd been up to, and make you pay in some small degree for what you'd done.'

Her lip curled. 'So that's why you told me about Sir Roger, and tried to frighten me.'

'I'm not proud of myself,' Gideon admitted quietly.

Harking back, she said, 'But then, presumably, you changed your mind? About bringing sex into it, I mean?'

'I couldn't resist the temptation to play a few games, to tease you a little, to find out what made you tick. Then suddenly I was hoist with my own petard; all I could think of was how much I wanted you.

'From your reactions I was sure you wanted me too, but for some reason—and I could only presume it was because I was David's uncle—you seemed determined to hold out.'

'So you plied me with brandy to lower my resistance.'

'My only excuse is that I thought you were…shall we say…a woman of the world. I thought your innocence was just a pretence. David had given me the impression that you were easy, and for a while I believed he was right.'

'Christmas afternoon, when you kissed me and I responded, you looked at me with a kind of contempt.'

'I had no right to—'

'Why not? I *was* easy,' she broke in, 'at least as far as you were concerned.'

He shook his head, 'You were no such thing. Even when I knew you were aroused, you fought your desire every step of the way—which, I must admit, surprised me. You see, David had told me you and he were living together, and your own story seemed to confirm it… That's why I was so shocked to find you were still a virgin.'

'Didn't you think it strange that he'd lied to you?'

'I presumed he'd been saving face. Reluctant to admit that a woman he'd spent so much money on was still holding out on him. David's always been a Casanova, not only able, but eager, to seduce any female who came along.'

'It seems to be a family trait.'

Gideon's mouth tightened ominously. Then he said quietly, 'I suppose in my father's case the accusation's justified.'

'But not in yours?'

'No, not in mine. I have many faults but that doesn't happen to be one of them. I don't mean there haven't been women in my life, but I'm certainly no Casanova. I've never gone in for one-night stands or cutting notches on the bedpost. I've never had more than one partner at a time. And I've never, until now, seduced an unwilling woman.'

Hearing the shame and regret in his voice, she felt a pang. Knowing she must ease his conscience, she said, 'But I wasn't *unwilling*.'

He sighed. 'Thank you for that.'

'I'm not just being kind. I don't think any woman can be seduced who isn't, to some extent, willing to be. I accept that what happened was my own fault. You're not to blame.' Flushing a little, she added, 'I was a consenting partner. I'm a grown woman, and I *wanted* you to make love to me.'

'Why? After keeping all your would-be lovers at bay until now, what was different about me?'

I loved you. The colour along her high cheekbones deepening, she spoke less than the truth. 'I found you very…attractive.'

'You must have found David attractive, in fact you told me that he turned you on, yet you held out against him.'

'As you remarked last night, I'm twenty-four now. Perhaps I decided it was high time I stopped being a virgin. In any case nothing can be changed.'

'I agree that it's too late to change anything, and I can't give you back your virginity, but—'

'As I've already told you, I wouldn't want it back... And I certainly don't want your kindness.'

'I'm not offering you kindness. I'm offering you marriage.'

For a moment she was stunned, then she laughed incredulously. '*Marriage!* Isn't that taking "making amends" a little *too* far?'

'It has nothing to do with making amends. You've just admitted that you find me attractive,' he pursued levelly, 'and I'm happy to give you the kind of commitment you've been looking for.'

Lifting her chin proudly, she said, 'Thanks, but no thanks.'

His jaw tightened. 'Don't refuse until you've thought about it.'

'I have thought about it,' she told him dismissively, 'and I don't want to marry you. You've done the "decent" thing, by offering, and I've refused. So now your conscience should be clear. There's no need to give it another thought.'

'There may be every need. Have you considered the possible consequences of what happened?'

'The possible consequences?' she echoed.

'You could be pregnant,' he said bluntly. 'Last night, thinking you were experienced, I presumed that you'd be protected.'

Momentarily, shock hit her, then, lifting her chin, she said valiantly, 'I *am* protected, so there's no need for concern.'

For a few seconds he studied her transparent face, then he shook his head. 'You're lying.'

Knowing it was useless to go on protesting, she admitted, 'All right, so I'm *not* protected. But if I do happen to be pregnant, which is most unlikely, I'll cope.'

'You mean get rid of it?'

'I don't mean any such thing! I wouldn't dream of getting rid of it!'

'Then you'll need a husband.'

'I don't want you to marry me just because I *might* be pregnant—'

'It's not just because—'

Ignoring the interruption, she swept on, 'If I am having a baby, I'll keep it, and take care of it, and love it. *On my own.*'

'Don't be a fool,' he said roughly. Then, in a softer tone, 'Look, if you do happen to be pregnant, you'll need my help. It takes more than love to bring up a baby. It takes money... And a father is no bad thing...'

'I don't want your help. I don't want your money. And I certainly don't want you to marry me just to make amends or salve your conscience!'

He jumped to his feet, and, seizing her upper arms, hauled her out of the chair and shook her slightly. 'It's nothing to do with making amends or salving my conscience. I'm asking you to marry me because I *want* to marry you—'

'I don't believe you,' she whispered hoarsely.

He sighed. 'It's my own fault. I was a fool. I shouldn't have asked you in the way I did, and I shouldn't have attempted to pressure you. If I'd let some time pass, tried to make friends with you first... But fools rush in where angels fear to tread, and I was terrified of losing you.'

Because it hurt so much, she cried, 'I don't want to listen to your lies!'

Sitting down in the chair, he pulled her on to his lap. She tried to struggle free, but he refused to let her go. 'They're not lies, and you're going to listen.'

She sat stiffly, face averted, hands clenched into fists, holding herself away from him.

'Even at the start, when I thought so badly of you, it was

instant enchantment. Though I tried not to admit it, I wanted you for myself, and I was furiously jealous when I thought of you sleeping with David...'

Taking the hand that was wearing the ring he'd given her, Gideon unfolded Anna's fingers one at a time and kissed each of them in turn. 'I swear that's the truth. Now I want to get things off my chest, so will you listen to the rest?'

Seeing her nearly imperceptible nod, he went on, 'When I knew my plan to keep you at the Manor was going to work, I rang Jackie and asked her to come over the following day. But almost at once I discovered you weren't at all the kind of woman I'd been expecting, and instead of blaming you I began to make excuses for you, to try and justify what I thought you'd done. I told myself that even decent people will go to great lengths to make their dreams come true. More than ready to forgive you, I tried to get you to admit the truth, to bring things into the open so we could get on to a different footing, and I was angry when you'd have none of it.

'You see, by this time I knew that, no matter what, I wanted to marry you. I also knew I didn't want to involve Jackie. But when I rang to stop her coming, I found she was already on her way, and David had opted to come with her to collect the cheque I'd promised him... I made one last attempt to pressure you into admitting the truth before they got here, but when you continued to play the innocent, I decided I had no option but to ask Jackie to identify you, and take it from there. When I found I'd been completely wrong about you, at first all I could feel was relief and gladness that you were as innocent as you seemed. Then I was racked by shame and guilt for the way I'd treated you. Finally fear took over. I was afraid that you might be unable to forgive me, afraid you'd leave me.

'I tried to tell myself that you wouldn't go. That you had

to feel *something* for me, otherwise you wouldn't have gone to bed with me last night, and you certainly wouldn't have agreed to go on with the relationship this morning. But when you asked Jackie to drop you off in town, and appeared so determined to leave, I wondered if I'd made yet another bad mistake. I might have stood by and allowed you to walk away, if Jackie hadn't suddenly remarked that I'd be a fool to let you go.

'She said, "As soon as I got here, you told me that no matter what Anna had done, you wanted to marry her. I presume that now she's been proved innocent you haven't changed your mind?" I told her, of course I hadn't. She said, "In that case try telling *her* how you feel."'

He used a single finger to turn Anna's face to his. 'You're the only woman I've ever felt this way about.'

Her heart beating in slow, heavy thuds, she asked, 'What about Eva? What happened to her?'

'In the end she went back to her husband. No, I wasn't broken-hearted. In fact by then, though I was fond of her, I was almost relieved. You see, she loved her husband a great deal more than she would ever have loved me, and somehow a second-best relationship wouldn't do. I want to love and *be* loved, deeply, passionately. That's why I was hoping that this *enchantment* I feel, for want of a better description, is mutual.'

'What better description could there be?'

'I understand the French call it a "*coup de foudre*". And even if it does sound a little hackneyed, we call it *love at first sight*. Though in spite of Christopher Marlowe some people may not even believe in it…'

'I do,' she said softly.

'Ah, but have you ever *experienced* it?'

'Just once. I thought I had once before, but I'd confused it with infatuation. This time there's no mistake.'

'Certain?'

'Quite certain.'

Gideon touched his lips enticingly to the corner of her mouth. 'I'd like to hear you tell me in so many words.'

'I love you.'

'Deeply?'

'Deeply.'

'Passionately?'

'Passionately. From the moment I set eyes on you.'

She was rewarded with a kiss that made her toes curl and her whole being glow with happiness.

'I feel the same way about you,' he told her.

For a while they kissed, lost in each other, then he raised his head to ask, 'So are you going to marry me and let me replace that fake solitaire on your finger with a real one?'

Looking at him from beneath long dark lashes, she said, 'I *might*.'

'What will it take to persuade you?'

'Well, I'd like the post you offered me as your secretary-cum-librarian…'

'It's yours.'

'And now I know how you feel about me, I'd like you to—' when she paused, blushing a little, he raised an interrogative brow '—make love to me again,' she finished in a rush.

'What, here and now?' he asked, straight-faced.

A little flustered, she said, 'If that's all right?'

Then, realising he was teasing her, blushing even harder, she pointed out, 'Well, I was a virgin for an awfully long time, so I feel I've some catching up to do.'

His grin wicked, he assured her, 'Don't worry, my love, I'm sure I can rise to the occasion.'

Harlequin Presents®
and
Harlequin Romance®
have come together to celebrate a year of royalty

 **By Royal Command**

EMOTIONALLY EXHILARATING!

Coming in June 2002
His Majesty's Marriage, #3703
Two original short stories by Lucy Gordan and Rebecca Winters

On-sale July 2002
The Prince's Proposal, #3709
by Sophie Weston

Seduction and Passion Guaranteed!

Coming in August 2002
Society Weddings, #2268
Two original short stories by Sharon Kendrick and Kate Walker

On-sale September 2002
The Prince's Pleasure, #2274
by Robyn Donald

**Escape into the exclusive world of royalty with
our royally themed books**

Available wherever Harlequin books are sold.

Visit us at www.eHarlequin.com

HPRROY

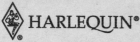

Harlequin invites you to experience the
charm and delight of

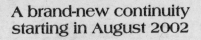

COOPER'S CORNER

A brand-new continuity
starting in August 2002

HIS BROTHER'S BRIDE
by *USA Today* bestselling author
Tara Taylor Quinn

Check-in: TV reporter Laurel London and noted travel
writer William Byrd are guests at the new Twin Oaks
Bed and Breakfast in Cooper's Corner.

Checkout: William Byrd suddenly vanishes and while
investigating, Laurel finds herself face-to-face with
policeman Scott Hunter. Scott and Laurel face a painful past.
Can cop and reporter mend their heartbreak and get to the
bottom of William's mysterious disappearance?

HARLEQUIN®
Makes any time special®